William Dawes

Samuel Adams

Thomas Paine

Paul Revere

John Hancock

Freedom at Any Price

March 1775 – April 19, 1775

By Amanda Stephens

Illustrated by the Flying Carnies

Grosset & Dunlap • New York

FIC
STE

Liberty's Kids ™ and © 2003 DIC Entertainment Corporation.
Published by Grosset & Dunlap, a division of Penguin Young Readers Group,
345 Hudson Street, New York, NY 10014.
GROSSET & DUNLAP is a trademark of Penguin Group (USA) Inc. Published simultaneously
in Canada. Printed in the U.S.A.
The 'See it on PBS KIDS' logo is a trademark of the
Public Broadcasting Service and is used with permission.
Library of Congress Cataloging-in-Publication Data is available.

ISBN 0-448-43247-1   A B C D E F G H I J

27- 8781

⋆ The Thirteen Colonies ⋆

New Hampshire
(1679)

Massachusetts
(1620)

New York
(1664)

Rhode Island
(1636)

Connecticut
(1639)

Pennsylvania
(1664)

New Jersey
(1664)

Delaware
(1682)

Virginia
(1607)

Maryland
(1632)

North Carolina
(1665)

South Carolina
(1670)

Georgia
(1729)

February 1775

Dearest Mother,

The mood in the colonies has turned ugly. Parliament has placed the port of Boston under blockade as punishment for the "Boston Tea Party." With the harbor closed to trade, the subjects of Boston are idle and suffer greatly.

Tensions are on the rise. Dr. Franklin's printing press is working round the clock to keep up with all these events.

I promise to write more when time permits.

Your loving daughter,
Sarah

Chapter One

Sarah Phillips, a tall, redheaded English girl with bright green eyes, sat quietly in her room in Philadelphia, writing a letter to her mother. Writing home always filled Sarah with emotion. As her quill scratched against the paper, Sarah's mind filled with images of London—the theaters, the stores, and especially her mother's warm smile and gentle touch. Her mother never seemed more far away than while Sarah was writing to her.

And the teenage girl was *very* far from home. It had taken Sarah nearly two months to sail from London to the colonies. Now she was staying at Dr. Benjamin Franklin's house in Philadelphia. Sarah's mother,

Lady Phillips, was a close friend of Dr. Franklin's, and the great statesman had been more than pleased to give Sarah a place to stay until her father could call for his family.

Sarah's father, Major Phillips, was an explorer. Currently he was traveling around the Ohios in service to King George III of England. It had been some time since Sarah had heard from him. It was very difficult for him to send her letters from the west. Thinking of her father and mother never ceased to make her a bit homesick.

While London was definitely the place she called home, Sarah had to admit that being in the Americas right now was an amazing opportunity. Everything was changing so rapidly within the colonies. Ever since the British had closed off Boston Harbor, the colonists had become more united against British rule.

They had formed a Continental Congress, made up of representatives from each of the thirteen colonies. The Congress was a place where the leaders of the individual colonies could discuss issues all the colonies had in common.

Sarah considered herself a loyal British citizen and, as such, she couldn't bring herself to agree with all the cries for revolution she heard on the streets of

Philadelphia. But she did appreciate that being in America right now was giving her a front-row seat to changes that would make history.

Sarah often got to hear about those changes before anyone else. That was one of the privileges that came with living in Dr. Franklin's house. Sarah's room was directly over the print shop where Dr. Franklin's newspaper, *The Pennsylvania Gazette*, was published.

But living above the print shop wasn't always wonderful. The old machines clanked and clunked all day long, and often into the night. There never seemed to be any peace and quiet in the house. Sometimes a girl needed a little quiet—even an adventurous girl like Sarah Phillips.

☆ ☆ ☆

"Moses! It did it again!" James Hiller shouted angrily as he yanked a shredded sheet of newsprint from the old printing press. The young apprentice was covered almost head to toe with black ink, but he had barely printed any newspapers.

A tall, muscular African-American man named Moses entered the room. Moses had also been hard at work, trying to get the latest edition of *The Pennsylvania Gazette* published. Like James, Moses worked for Dr. Franklin. His official title was major-domo, meaning someone who took care of the household. Since Dr. Franklin was in England at the moment, Moses was in charge.

"This ol' thing is a hunk of junk!" James moaned. He banged his fist on the press handle. The handle snapped around—and whacked James in the back of the head. "How are we supposed to get out the latest news from Boston if our press keeps breaking down?"

Moses didn't answer. He was used to the teenage boy's tirades. James was an excitable boy. Talented, for sure. But impulsive as well.

"James," Moses replied in a cool, calm voice, "this poor old press is ready for retirement." He gently rubbed the excess ink from the side of the machine. "However, I have just the fix," he added.

"Great!" James exclaimed as he headed for the toolbox. "What do you need? A wrench? A hammer? I'll fetch it for you."

"A wagon," Moses told him.

James stopped mid step. "A what?"

"A big, sturdy wagon," Moses assured him. "I made an offer on a new press. We just have to pick it up!"

"Great!" James was nearly exploding with excitement. "Where is it? Market Street?"

Moses shook his head. "Williamsburg."

"Williamsburg?" James stopped for a moment. There was no Williamsburg Street in Philadelphia. Then, suddenly, he realized where Moses meant. "Williamsburg, Virginia?" he asked.

"We leave at the first light of day," Moses told him.

That didn't seem like a great idea to James. It was too dangerous for Moses to go to Virginia. "But . . . but—" the teen stammered.

"But nothing," Moses interrupted. "We must have a dependable press. The people count on us for their news. Besides, you never can tell what news you'll uncover in a different colony."

Ordinarily, that would have been enough to grab James's interest. The boy was, after all, an apprentice on a newspaper. His goal was to someday be a full-fledged reporter for the *Gazette*. But now he was concerned more for Moses than anything else. "Is it safe?" he asked him. "I mean, for you? Slavery is everywhere in Virginia. It's not at all like Boston—or even here in Pennsylvania."

Moses nodded slowly. He knew what James meant. Moses was lucky to be a free man in Pennsylvania.

But there was a time when he himself had been a slave in Virginia, as had his brother. Moses had worked hard as a blacksmith and had earned enough in tips from his customers to purchase his own freedom. He'd traveled to Pennsylvania and gone to work with Dr. Franklin, a man who hated slavery as much as he did.

But other African Americans hadn't been quite as fortunate. Moses didn't even know where his brother was now. And while Dr. Franklin believed in freedom for all, there weren't many men like him in southern colonies like Virginia. Still . . .

"These are dangerous times for everyone," Moses said finally. "And I'm willing to do what I can for the common cause."

James listened intently, but he wasn't convinced. Moses would be taking an awfully big chance. There was no telling what could happen to an African-American man in the South.

"I won't be without protection," Moses assured James. He pulled a piece of writing paper from his pocket. "I have this letter from Dr. Franklin. It attests that I am a free man. I carry it with me always."

James looked at Moses with admiration. The man never ceased to amaze him. "Moses, if the colonies had ten thousand men as brave as you, Parliament wouldn't dare mess with us!" James praised him.

Moses smiled. "Speaking of mess," he joked, pointing toward James's ink-stained face.

"Right," James agreed. "Where's the soap?"

"You don't know?" Moses asked curiously.

"Well, let's see. I used it last Saturday . . ." James began.

Moses sniffed at the air around the teenager. "More like last January," he said, making a face.

James frowned. "Maybe it was two Saturdays ago," he said.

Before James could search for the soap, Sarah walked into the printing room. She was followed by a small, mischievous, eight-year-old French boy. Like James, Henri Lefebvre was an apprentice in the print shop. *Unlike* James, he wasn't anxious to be a reporter. He was usually more interested in filling his tummy.

"Still working?" Sarah asked James and Moses. She looked out the window at the dark street. "At this hour?"

James was excited to see the other kids. He couldn't wait to tell them the news. James loved adventures, and he was about to go on a big one. "Sarah! Henri!

Big news. I'm going with Moses to Virginia to buy a new printing press!" he boasted.

But Sarah and Henri didn't sound as excited as James. In fact, they seemed rather upset.

"And leave me alone with her?" Henri exclaimed.

"And leave me alone with him?" Sarah demanded.

"I'm going with you!" they both shouted out at the exact same time. James didn't know what to do. He didn't want either of them to go along. He and Moses would be just fine on their own. "Moses! Help!" he shouted. Moses sighed. The only way to make everyone happy was to take all three kids along on the adventure. He hadn't planned on having so many passengers in the wagon as he made the journey south. Still, Sarah, James, and Henri were all responsible kids who always volunteered to be of help. And Moses had learned a long time ago that you never knew when you might be in need of a little help.

Chapter Two

The very next morning, Moses, James, Henri, and Sarah left for Virginia. But this was no pleasure trip. It was hard work navigating the roads heading south from Philadelphia.

"I hope this new press is worth the money, Moses," James remarked, grunting as he gave Dr. Franklin's wagon an extra hard push up the hill. The roads to Virginia were old and muddy. It was hard to get the wagon uphill. It needed an extra push—one provided by Moses, James, and Henri. They stood behind the wagon, using all their muscles to move the wagon along. Only Sarah got to ride. Someone had to hold the horse's reins, after all.

"As Dr. Franklin said, 'A penny saved is a penny earned,'" Moses reminded him. "This press will save us a very pretty penny."

"How much longer till Williamsburg?" Sarah called back to Moses.

"Yeah, I'm hungry," Henri piped up.

James scowled. "You're always hungry." He turned to Moses. "I hope we get there in time for the session of the House of Burgesses," he said, referring to the Virginia legislature. "I want to hear Patrick Henry speak."

"Patrick who?" Henri asked.

"Patrick Henry. He's a lawyer from Virginia," James told him. He sounded proud to be able to share the information he'd learned while reporting on the congressional meetings back in Philadelphia. "He was a delegate to the First Continental Congress, and what a speaker! The finest I've ever heard. He's a modern-day Demosthenes!"

Now Henri was really confused. "Demo-what's it?" he asked.

"Demosthenes was the greatest speaker in the world," Moses explained. "In ancient Greece, he rallied the Athenians to rise up against Philip and Alexander of Macedonia."

That caught Sarah's attention. "Don't tell me Patrick Henry is a rebel!" she exclaimed. Sarah felt a loyalty to England and King George that James didn't share.

"He's not a rebel, Sarah," James barked back. "He's a patriot. "He wants the Southern colonies to join the common cause with New England."

Sarah rolled her eyes. "Why would a subject of Virginia care what's happening in Massachusetts? It's a completely different country."

"With men like Patrick Henry," James assured her, "it might just become one country."

Before Sarah could argue that in her mind they were already all part of one country—that country being England—her eyes discovered something in the distance. "Look! A farm!" she shouted out as she pulled back on the horses' reins.

Instantly, the wagon came to a stop. James, Henri, and Moses didn't stop, however. Instead, they smashed right into the rear of the wagon.

"Sarah, please don't do that again," Moses called up to her.

"But I see a farm," Sarah explained. "Just ahead! Those workers will know how much farther it is to Williamsburg."

Moses looked at the farm. A big white house with huge pillars stood at the entrance to the farm. Behind it were rows and rows of neatly manicured crops. Workers with farm equipment tended the crops, under the watchful eye of a foreman on horseback.

Moses looked out over the plantation. His eyes grew sad, remembering. "We won't be stopping at that farm, Sarah," he said slowly.

"Why not?"

"Because those workers aren't just workers. They're slaves."

Moses, James, and Henri climbed back into the wagon. Sarah shook the reins, and the horses moved on. They traveled in silence.

☆ ☆ ☆

As Moses and the children rode through the Virginia colony, Benjamin Franklin was about to begin a journey of his own. He was preparing to return home to Philadelphia. He'd spent quite a while in England, trying to negotiate with Parliament for fair treatment for the colonies. But Parliament seemed determined to tax the colonists for just about everything—without giving the Americans any say. And now, Dr. Franklin himself was being called a traitor to England.

That title didn't bother Dr. Franklin a bit. He no longer considered himself English, anyway. He thought of himself as an American. And now, he was going home. But before he could do that, he wanted to say good-bye to his dear friend Lady Phillips.

"Dr. Franklin, you're leaving us?" Lady Phillips asked as she led him into her library, a room filled with books on every subject. The beautifully furnished room never ceased to impress Dr. Franklin. He, too, was an avid reader.

"The rumor is true, Lady Phillips," Benjamin Franklin admitted as he took a seat across from her. "As soon as I tie up my affairs here in London, I will return to my home. To Philadelphia. To America."

"Oh Doctor, you will be missed," Lady Phillips assured him.

Ben Franklin wasn't so sure. "By my friends, perhaps. But my enemies are in far greater number, and if they shed tears upon my departure, they shall be tears of joy. What word have you from your lovely daughter Sarah?"

"She's off on a trip. To Williamsburg, which is the capital of Virginia, I believe."

"Does she say why?" Dr. Franklin asked. "I haven't had a letter in some weeks now."

"Something about buying a new printing press," Lady Phillips recalled. "It makes no sense to me, Doctor. This new world where women are involved in all sorts of odd things! I take comfort in knowing she's in the company of your people—James, Henri, and your majordomo, Moses."

Ben's eyes widened with alarm. "Moses, did you say?"

"Is there something wrong?" Lady Phillips asked nervously.

"Perhaps not," Ben tried to console her. Then, under his breath, he added, "But perhaps so."

Chapter Three

Williamsburg was a very different city than the children were used to back home in Pennsylvania. Philadelphia was a city of cobblestone streets, wooden houses, and stores, with people hustling and bustling along Market Street.

Williamsburg was more like the English countryside, with huge, white brick homes, and lush gardens through which finely dressed men and women went strolling. It was also a city filled with exciting scents and smells—especially to someone with as keen a nose as Henri.

Williamsburg

"I smell ham!" the eight-year-old exclaimed as the wagon rolled into the city. "I also smell mutton, roast beef, pudding, and pie. I love Williamsburg."

James laughed. "I swear, Henri, you're part bloodhound."

Sarah was also impressed with the Southern city. "It is quite beautiful," she remarked in her proper British accent. "These Southerners are obviously well bred."

But looks can be deceiving. Not everything in Williamsburg was beautiful. In fact, some of the goings-on were quite ugly. And as soon as the wagon reached the Market Square, the kids came face-to-face with that ugliness.

There was an auction going on in the center of the square. A stage had been set up, where the auctioneer was doing his job. Behind the stage was a pen—almost like the kind you would keep animals in. Except this pen held grown men—slaves, who were being auctioned off to the highest bidder.

Sarah almost lost her breath as she watched one of the men being put on display. "Oh, my goodness!" she gasped. "Is that . . ."

"Yes, Sarah. The auction block," Moses told her, his face brimming with a combination of sorrow and rage. "This is where my people are auctioned off to the highest bidder. I was sold on the block in Charlestown, South Carolina. But they're all the same."

Sarah's face had taken on an even more angry expression than Moses's. "It's barbaric!" she exclaimed. "I can not look at it. Not another second." She turned her head and tried to block the auction from her brain. But she could still hear the auctioneer, and she knew she'd never forget the sight of those men being sold. "I want to leave this place," she added quietly.

"The newspaper office is right across the street," James assured her. "Come on, Moses. Let's pick up the printing press and get out of here."

Moses shook his head. "No, James. You're a reporter. You have a job to do. I'll get the printing press. You get yourself over to the House of Burgesses and find out the latest news."

"But—" James began to argue.

"No buts." Moses cut him off. "Each of us must do his part. You're a reporter, so report."

"Is it safe for you here?" Sarah asked Moses nervously.

Moses patted his jacket pocket. "As long as I have

this letter, I'll be fine," he assured her.

James knew that there was no changing Moses's mind once he'd made a decision.

"Come on, Henri," the teen said as he leaped from the wagon. Henri did as he was told. He jumped from the wagon and landed on the ground beside James. As Moses and Sarah drove off, James spotted a peddler pushing his food cart through the street. The cart was brimming with meat and pies. James reached into his pocket for a coin. "Do you want something to eat?" he asked Henri.

Henri wrinkled his nose and shook his head. "No," he said quietly. "Suddenly I've lost my appetite."

James looked back toward the slave auction. He knew exactly what Henri meant. Quickly, the boys turned and headed off toward the House of Burgesses. The sooner James got the information he needed for his article, the sooner they could go back to Philadelphia.

Unfortunately, when James and Henri arrived at the impressive red brick building that housed the Virginia legislature, they found the gates locked.

"That's strange," James remarked.

"In the middle of the day?" Henri added.

James thought for a moment. He needed to hear

what was going on inside the building. He wasn't going to let something like a lock keep him from his mission. Quickly he scrambled up the iron gate. When he got to the top, he reached his hand down for Henri to grab. "Up you go," James told the younger boy.

Henri took hold of James's hand. James yanked his arm back, to pull Henri up. But James didn't know his own strength. He pulled so hard, the two boys tumbled over the gate. They landed with a crash.

"Ouch," James moaned, rubbing his scalp.

"Lucky for me I landed on your head," Henri told him.

James moaned slightly and scrambled to his feet. Slowly, he opened the doors and walked inside the House of Burgesses.

Ordinarily, there would be representatives seated at the tables that dotted the room. They would be writing with their quill pens, raising their hands to speak, even arguing.

But today, no representatives were there at all. Just two slave women. One mopped the floor while the other dusted the tables.

"Where is everybody?" James asked one of the women.

"Gone."

"Gone?" Henri asked, surprised. "Gone where?"

"Gone away," the woman answered flatly. "There is no more House of Burgesses. The earl of Dunmore shut it down."

"The earl of who?" Henri asked.

"The earl of Dunmore," James explained. "He's the royal governor of Virginia."

The slave woman nodded. "That's right. He got mighty mad at the assembly, especially at Mr. Patrick Henry for saying Virginia should raise an army to fight with the Boston people."

James eyes brightened. He pulled his charcoal and paper from his coat pocket. "Now that's news!" he exclaimed. "Are you sure?"

The woman smiled. "I hear everything," she confided to James. "Rumor has it Mr. Henry's going to speak to a convention in Richmond. St. John's Church."

The woman stopped and looked around nervously. "But if anybody asks, you didn't hear it from me."

"That's fantastic!" James said, scribbling notes as quickly as he could. "Thanks . . ." He paused for a moment. "What is your name?"

The woman shook her head and moved away from James. "Oh no. I've said too much already," she said fearfully.

James put his pad and charcoal away and raced

for the door. "Wait till Moses hears this!" he told Henri. Then he turned toward the slave woman who had been so helpful. "Thank you," he shouted as he raced off to tell Moses the news.

$$\star \quad \star \quad \star$$

Chapter Four

$$\star \quad \star \quad \star$$

"Moses! Big news!" James shouted as he raced down the street toward the local newspaper office. In the distance he could already see Moses and another man hoisting the printing press into the wagon. "We've got to go to Richmond," James huffed. The words tumbled from his mouth as he struggled to catch his breath. "The earl of Dunmore sent the assembly home! But they're going to meet, anyway, in Richmond! Patrick Henry is going to make an important speech. We have to be there, Moses. This is news! Huge news!"

James's unbridled enthusiasm made Henri laugh.

"I'm so excited, I have to lie down," he teased. The mischievous eight-year-old hopped into the wagon, placed his hand to his forehead, and dramatically dropped to the floor.

Moses smiled at Henri's inspired performance, but the importance of what James had just said wasn't lost on him. The African-American man climbed aboard the wagon and took the reins. "If we're going to hear that speech, we'd better get going," he said.

At that, James jumped into the back of the wagon. With a single shake of the reins, the horse began to move. The wagon was moving slower now, under the weight of the new press. It was harder work for the horse. James knew that, of course, but he was still impatient. He couldn't wait to get to Richmond. "If the protest against Parliament spreads to the Southern colonies, there's no telling how far this might go!" he told Moses.

But Moses barely heard him. His attention was focused elsewhere. There was look of total shock—and horror—on his face. Quickly, he yanked on the reins and drew the horse to a stop.

"What's wrong, Moses?" Sarah asked.

Moses pointed to a young African-American man who was being led to an auction platform by two greedy slave traders.

"It's awful," James agreed. "He looks scared."

At first, Moses didn't say a word. His whole body seemed consumed by anger and sadness. The suddenly, he said, "He's my brother."

At first, the children weren't sure they'd heard him correctly. "He's your *brother*?" James asked incredulously.

Moses nodded. "His name is Cato. We were separated when we were young. But I'd know him anywhere."

Sarah jumped to attention. "We have to do something!" she declared.

"Yes," Henri agreed. "But what?"

Sarah thought for a moment. "We can buy his freedom," she suggested.

James shook his head. "With what?" he wondered. "We spent all our money on the printing press."

"I have some coins," Sarah volunteered. She sighed, knowing full well that would never be enough to buy freedom for Moses's younger brother.

But a lack of funds wasn't going to stop Moses. "I'll sell this horse and wagon and carry the press home on my back if I must, but I'll not sit here while Cato is sold like a sack of flour!" he declared. He leaped down from the wagon and began hurrying toward the auction block. James, Sarah, and Henri followed close behind.

The auction was painful for the children to watch.

A Slave Auction

Cato was shoved like a piece of meat into the center of the platform. His face was filled with fury as the auctioneer stepped forward and began speaking to the crowd of white Southern men who had gathered around.

"Our next item is a healthy, well-formed Negro in his early twenties. He's a captured runaway, high-spirited, so he'll have to be watched carefully. But he's strong as a mule, with good teeth, and there's plenty of work to be had from him." He smiled at the crowd. "Who'll start the bidding?"

"Fifty pounds!" A thick-waisted plantation foreman named Harrison shouted out.

"I have fifty pounds," the auctioneer called, scouting the crowd with his eye. "Do I hear sixty?"

"Sixty pounds!" Moses's voice rang out loud and strong.

"I have sixty, do I hear seventy?" the auctioneer asked, not caring who had made the bid.

But Harrison cared very much who was bidding against him. And when he saw that the bid had come from an African American, his face turned red with anger. "Stop the auction!" the plantation foreman shouted. "This is most peculiar."

The crowd grew silent and watched as Harrison

stalked over toward Moses and stared him straight in the eye. "Have you no respect?" Harrison demanded. "Negroes ain't allowed to bid at auction."

But Moses would not back down. "My offer stands," he declared. "Sixty pounds, cash money."

"This is outrageous!" Harrison barked. "You should be *up there* yourself, not down here. The nerve!"

"The man you are selling is my brother, Cato," Moses replied, refusing to let the man intimidate him. "I am a free man and have as much right to bid as any."

"He speaks the truth, sir," Sarah added, summing up all the courage she had.

"Quiet, child," Harrison demanded. "It's bad enough I'm talkin' with a Negro. I'll not stoop to discussing my affairs with a girl to boot!"

"I'd like to give *him* the boot," Henri whispered to James.

"Moses *is* a free man," James told Harrison. "Show him your letter, Moses."

Moses reached into his jacket pocket and produced the letter from Dr. Franklin. He held the paper proudly in his hands so Harrison could see it.

Harrison squinted his eyes and struggled with the print. It was obvious he had difficulty reading.

"It's from my employer, Dr. Benjamin Franklin," Moses told Harrison.

The plantation foreman scowled. "I don't need no read'n less'ns from no Negro," he snapped.

Cato watched the scene from the auction block. His eyes were brimming with hope that his brother could somehow pull off this miracle and set him free.

But that was not to be. Harrison lifted his riding crop and whipped right through the letter from Dr. Franklin, tearing it in half. "Ben Franklin's name don't mean nothin' in Virginia," he declared, his lips curling into a snarl. "He's a Pennsylvania man. And if you belongs to him, I suggest you git, pronto. And I do mean pronto."

Moses looked from the torn letter to his brother and then to Harrison. He was livid. Every muscle in his body seemed to be tensing at once. Without thinking, he curled his fingers into a huge fist and got ready to swing.

"Moses! No!" Cato shouted from the auction platform.

A group of white men raced in and grabbed Moses from behind. "Get him out of here!" Harrison told them. He watched as Moses was dragged away. "My bid stands at fifty pounds," the foreman added triumphantly.

The auctioneer nodded. "Fifty pounds," he agreed. "Going once, going twice. Sold to Foreman Harrison of the Abernathy Plantation, Richmond, Virginia."

"Richmond!" James exclaimed. "That's where Patrick Henry is speaking. Come on!"

The children raced to Moses's side. "Moses! Cato was sold to the Abernathy Plantation . . ." James began.

"In Richmond," Sarah continued. "We are going to Richmond, aren't we Moses?"

Moses's jaw was set with determination. "As if we had wings," he assured Sarah as he leaped into the wagon. Within seconds, the group was on its way.

Chapter Five

Moses and the children traveled throughout the night, refusing to stop until they reached Richmond. The wagon moved along the country roads of Virginia as fast as the horse could carry it. There was no time to waste.

From the moment they arrived in Richmond it was obvious that this small city was not at all like Williamsburg. Here, the houses were made of wood, not brick, and the roads weren't paved.

As the wagon passed by a small country church, James looked at the sign on the door. "There's St. John's Church," he told the others. "That's where Mr. Henry's going to speak."

Moses brought the horse to a stop. He leaped out of the wagon and left James, Henri, and Sarah to tend to the weary horse. In the meantime, Moses headed over to a group of men who were filing into the church.

The children watched as Moses spoke to the men. Within a few minutes he returned to the wagon, more determined than ever to find his brother. "The Abernathy Plantation is just outside town. We passed it coming in." He leaned in close and whispered his plan to them. He had no intention of driving the wagon to the plantation. And he had no plans to bring the children with him, either. "I'll draw less attention on foot," he explained. "Meet Cato and me here after dark."

"Please let us go with you, Moses," Sarah pleaded, her voice filled with concern for his safety.

Moses shook his head. "This is family, Sarah. I have to do this for my brother." He looked encouragingly at James. "Now make sure you get down every word Patrick Henry says. The colonies need to hear a man like Mr. Henry."

James nodded. "We won't let you down, Moses."

Moses was certain of that. He forced a brave smile to his lips. "Good," he said. "Till we meet again."

And with that, he turned and went back down the road in the direction of the Abernathy Plantation.

Henri looked up at the two teenagers. "Are you gonna just let him go?" he asked them nervously.

Sarah looked down at a piece of torn paper. "James!" she shouted as she picked it up. "Look! His letter!"

James stared at the letter. They had to get it to Moses. But they'd promised him that they would record Patrick Henry's speech. They couldn't all do both, but . . .

"It doesn't take three of us to copy down a speech," James noted.

"And I can hardly write my name!" Henri admitted.

"True. But you are a world-class sneak," James told him. "Henri, you tail Moses. But keep your distance so he doesn't know he's being followed."

Sarah looked Henri straight in the eye. "But at the first sign of trouble, fly back here and get us. Do you understand?"

Henri rolled his eyes. "Maybe I can't write English, but I understand plenty," he assured her.

"Good. Then get going," James commanded. "Moses has enough of a head start."

As Henri raced off after Moses, James turned to

Sarah. It was time for him to fulfill their commitment to the newspaper . . . and to Moses. "Come on," he said. "Let's find a seat inside."

Sarah followed James inside the church and sat down right beside him. She reached into her bag and pulled out a pencil and a notebook of paper. James stared at her. "What are you doing with a pencil?" he demanded.

"Two heads are better than one," Sarah replied matter-of-factly. "Especially when one of the heads is yours."

"But *you're* not a reporter," he insisted.

"Shhhh!" Sarah scolded, putting her finger to her lips. Her eyes moved toward the front of the room. "Mr. Patrick Henry."

James looked up to see a good-looking, well-dressed man in his late thirties stand and walk toward the front of the church, preparing to address the members of the House of Burgesses. As he took his place before the members of the House of Burgesses, the men in the audience grew so silent, you could hear a pin drop.

And then, Patrick Henry began his speech. "The question before the house is one of awful moment to this country," he told the representatives. "For my own part, I consider this as nothing less than a question of freedom or slavery. There is no longer any room for hope. If we wish to be free, if we mean to preserve those privileges for which we have been so long contending, we must fight!"

James and Sarah scribbled ferociously, each taking down every word the great orator spoke.

"I repeat it, sirs, we must fight!" Patrick Henry continued. "An appeal to arms and to the God of Hosts is all that is left us! They tell us we are weak, unable to cope with so formidable an adversary. But when shall we be stronger?"

The members of the House of Burgesses seemed to be under some sort of spell as Patrick Henry gave his address. They sat still and silent, soaking in his every word.

"Will it be next week or next year?" he continued. "We are not weak. We are three million people armed in the holy cause of liberty! Gentlemen may cry, 'Peace! Peace!' but there is no peace. The war is actually begun. The next gale that sweeps from Boston will bring to our ears the clash of resounding arms! Our brethren are already in the field! Why stand we here idle?"

"Is life so dear, or peace so sweet as to be purchased at the price of chains and slavery? Forbid it, Almighty God! I know not what course others may

Patrick Henry Addressing the House of Burgesses

take, but as for me, *give me liberty or give me death!*"

"Huzzah!" At that, the members of the Virginia House of Burgesses rose to their feet and cheered wildly. Patrick Henry had become their voice—the voice of freedom.

☆ ☆ ☆

Unfortunately that cry for freedom was of no help to Moses's brother Cato. He was trapped in slavery on the Abernathy Plantation. That very night he found himself in the slave quarters, along with other male slaves. The room was bare with no beds or blankets, only old rugs for the men to sleep on. A fire crackled in the fireplace. All around him, other slaves sang spirituals—praises to God. But Cato couldn't find it within himself to sing. He sat alone off to the side.

And that's where Moses found him after creeping onto the plantation grounds under the cover of night. It hadn't taken him long to find his brother's quarters.

"Moses!" Cato exclaimed as he discovered his brother. "What are you doing here?"

"I came to get you. To take you with me to Philadelphia."

Cato looked at Moses as though he had three

heads. Was he crazy? "No. It's too risky," he insisted.

"I'm not leaving you here!" Moses told his younger brother.

"Don't worry about me," Cato assured him. "I have a plan."

"A plan?" Moses asked.

Cato nodded. "There is a rumor—a strong rumor—from sources that are never wrong."

"What is it?"

"Lord Dunmore is going to offer freedom to any slave who joins the British to put down the rebellion in Boston," Cato confided.

Moses didn't seem as sure of that as Cato did. "But that's just talk," he told his brother. "I'm offering you a way out."

Cato shook his head. "You're offering me a life on the run, as a fugitive. I want freedom. The freedom every man should have. I'll not spend my life looking over my shoulder, waiting for bounty hunters to drag me back here in chains."

"But . . ." Moses interrupted.

Cato would not let him speak. He looked into his brother's eyes. "Moses, I love you," he said. "You are a brave man for coming here. But I will not live my life as if I were a criminal. The only 'crime' I'm guilty of is having the wrong skin color. If I can win my freedom by helping the British, so be it. At least I will be the master of my own fate."

Moses looked at his brother thoughtfully. "Are you sure?"

Cato nodded. "I've never been more sure."

Before another word could be spoken, the door to the cabin shot open. Harrison, the plantation foreman, and two other workers stormed into the room. The workers each had muskets at their sides.

"It's late!" Harrison barked as his eyes ominously scanned the room. "Stop that blasted singing!" He paused for a minute and stared at the two tall African-American men standing alone in the corner of the room. He recognized Moses almost immediately. "You!" he shouted. "Get him, boys!"

Before Moses could move, the plantation workers grabbed him by the arms. Moses's eyes blazed. He was captured, and there was no one there to help him.

★ ★ ★

At least, that's what Moses thought. But the truth was, there *was* someone there who could help.

Henri had been watching through the window. He'd seen everything. "I've got to get James and Sarah!" he exclaimed as he hurried off toward Richmond.

Chapter Six

Sarah and James walked out of St. John's Church feeling excited, and a little confused. Patrick Henry's speech had brought a lot of change. It was hard to take it all in.

"What does it all mean, James?" Sarah asked. "Is Virginia going to send an army to Boston?"

"Not unless fighting breaks out," James assured her. "But thanks to Patrick Henry, at least Virginia will have an army. The convention voted funds to buy weapons and uniforms and hire officers. This is a great day!"

Perhaps it was a great day for some people. But Henri had a completely different point of view. As soon as he spotted Sarah and James, he ran straight for them. "Jaaaames! Saaaaarah!" he shouted.

Sarah looked at James. "What now?"

Henri was out of breath by the time he reached the teens. He'd run the whole way from the Abernathy Plantation.

"Quick!" he huffed. "Moses has been taken by plantation men!"

"No!" Sarah exclaimed in horror.

James jumped to action. "Quick! The wagon!"

As the kids drove off toward the plantation, James could feel his heart pounding. Moses needed them, now more than ever. "We're coming, Moses!" he said to himself.

✷ ✷ ✷

Even with the heavy printing press in tow, it didn't take long for the wagon to reach the plantation. The Abernathy farm was just outside of town. As soon as the wagon pulled up to the main house, James leaped out and banged on the front door of the main house.

A heavyset man in his mid-fifties opened the door. Seeing James, Henri, and Sarah, he muttered, "May I help you?"

"We're looking for our friend," James said, trying to remain calm.

But Henri was making no such attempt. "Moses!"

he cried out frantically. "His name is Moses. Give him back!" The little guy put up his fists. It looked as though he was willing to fight a grown man for Moses's sake.

But James wasn't about to let that happen. He held the boy back.

"What makes you think I have your friend, this Moses character?"

"You have him!" Henri told the plantation owner. "I saw your foreman, Harrison, take him prisoner."

Now Mr. Abernathy understood. "The runaway caught stirring up trouble in my slave quarters? That's your *friend*?"

Something in the man's tone infuriated Sarah. "Yes sir, he is our friend," she assured him. "Only Moses isn't a runaway. He's a *free* man. See for yourself." She took Moses's torn letter from her pocket and shoved it in his face.

"What's this?" Mr. Abernathy demanded.

"That is a letter from Dr. Benjamin Franklin of Philadelphia—" James began.

"I am aware of Dr. Franklin," the plantation owner interrupted. "But why is this any of his business?"

"Because as a man of honor, you have no right to keep that which does not belong to you," Sarah informed him.

"And this Moses belongs to Dr. Franklin?"

James shook his head. "Moses belongs to *himself*."

"It's all there in black and white," Sarah added.

Before Mr. Abernathy could even read the letter, Harrison burst in. It was obvious he'd been asleep for a while. He was buttoning his shirt as he came through the door. "Is everything okay, Mr. Abernathy?" he asked. "I heard a wagon roll up . . ."

Mr. Abernathy nodded. "The Negro named Moses," he said, "where is he?"

Harrison smiled proudly. "I locked him in the blockhouse. His running days are over."

"Release him immediately," Mr. Abernathy said.

Harrison seemed surprised. "Release him?" he asked. "But . . ."

"Now, Harrison," Mr. Abernathy insisted, "our guests here have a long ride ahead of them." The plantation owner turned to James, Sarah, and Henri. His face did not look friendly. "Which I suggest you embark on posthaste," he added.

"So you believe us?" Sarah asked with surprise.

Mr. Abernathy sighed. "If Dr. Franklin is in the business of hiring Negroes, that's his business, not mine. Be off with you. But tell Dr. Franklin he's playing with lightning, again. His radical notions about slavery might fly in Philadelphia, but he'll set the world on fire if he tries to export them to Virginia. You make sure you tell him that."

"Oh, we will, sir," James assured him, not wanting to make any trouble. "We will."

"We'll be sure to tell him," Sarah agreed.

"As soon as he gets home from London," Henri continued. "You have our word."

Mr. Abernathy seemed to believe them. He would have been far less convinced, however, had he seen that all three children held crossed fingers behind their backs.

⋆ ⋆ ⋆

James, Henri, and Sarah did not relax until Moses was back in the wagon, and they were heading north. It had been a close call for their friend. But now, things seemed to be getting back to normal . . . or at least as normal as things can be when revolution is in the air.

When he finally felt safe, James pulled out his notebook and filled Moses in on the monumental speech Patrick Henry had made.

"And then Patrick Henry said, 'Give me liberty or give me death!'" James proclaimed, trying to mimic Patrick Henry's oratory style as he read through his notes.

"That's a mighty fine speech," Moses agreed. "Good job, James."

"It's a bunch of hogwash," Sarah differed.

"Hogwash? Sarah, it was greatness!" James argued.

But Sarah wouldn't change her mind. "All that talk of freedom and liberty," she scoffed. "Look what happened to Moses."

"And what about Cato?" Henri reminded James.

James thought about that for a moment. In all this excitement, they'd forgotten to ask. "Yeah. Moses, what *about* Cato?"

Moses pointed to a sign nailed to a tree. The children followed his finger. The sign read:

FREEDOM FOR SLAVES WHO TAKE
UP ARMS AGAINST THE COLONISTS

"It's signed by Lord Dunmore for his Majesty King George III!" Sarah read.

"Cato is taking his own path to freedom," Moses told the others. "If it's God's will, he'll succeed. I believe it is God's will. I believe someday all my people will drink from the cup of liberty, just like Patrick Henry said."

March 1775

Dearest Mother,

We have returned safely from Virginia, but not without a terrible fright and not without the blinders being lifted from my eyes. Whatever unity Mr. Patrick Henry was able to achieve by bringing the colony of Virginia into the cause with New England, this land shall remain divided as long as slavery remains the law.

It is an awful practice, degrading to the slave and to the master. It's an evil that should be stamped from the world wherever it lives. I've learned there are many paths to freedom. Moses took one path; his brother Cato, another. Just as England and the colonies are traveling different paths. My fear is, these paths are destined to collide. Freedom will not come cheaply. It never does.

Your loving daughter,
Sarah

Chapter Seven

Sarah adored spring in Philadelphia. Each day brought a new surprise: flowers blossoming on the trees, fresh fruits at the market, and longer, sunnier days.

But the spring had brought some not-so-wonderful surprises, as well. Most of those came in the form of protests from readers of *The Pennsylvania Gazette*.

Benjamin Franklin was committed to his newspaper business. He felt the *Gazette* was stirring patriotism in the bosom of every colonist.

Unfortunately, not everyone thought American patriotism was such a great idea. In fact, it seemed to Sarah that no two colonies shared the same interests.

To her, Pennsylvania and Virginia seemed as different as France and Holland. All the arguing made Sarah jumpy, which explains why she leaped out of bed one night in April, after being absolutely sure she'd heard noises coming from the hall.

Slowly, the brave teen snuck out into the darkened hallway. She didn't take a candle with her—she had no desire to bring attention to herself. But it didn't matter. Whoever was in the hall knew she was there. Suddenly, a long, strong arm reached out from behind and grabbed her, covering her mouth so she couldn't scream.

But Sarah tried, anyway, letting out nothing more than a muffled cry.

"Shhhh! It's me, James," the mysterious hall walker informed her.

Sarah took a deep breath as James released his grip on her. She turned to find Henri and James standing beside her.

"You heard the voices, too?" James asked her.

"I think it's thieves," Henri suggested.

"Or someone who disagrees with Mr. Franklin's newspaper," Sarah countered.

James had the same idea as Sarah. "They're here to destroy the printing presses!" he said. "Come on."

Without a thought for their own safety, the three

children ran down the stairs. Sure enough, they could the hear the presses running. Someone was in the print shop.

"I'll scare them off," Sarah whispered to James. "You trip them up."

"Run!" a strange voice called into the darkness. Suddenly there seemed to be a lot of movement in the room. One of the intruders vaulted over the counter and bolted out the door. A second man ran after him, going around the counter toward the door. Unfortunately, that was not as direct a route. In the darkness, the second intruder tripped over a stack of newsprint. He fell to the floor with a thud.

"We got 'em! We got 'em!" Henri shouted gleefully.

"One of 'em at least," James agreed. "Sarah, run and get Moses."

The intruder moaned. "No need to get Moses. You already got him."

Sarah held a candle close to the man's face. It was Moses all right.

"Moses! But why?" James asked. "Why all the sneaking around?"

Maybe he's a traitor and a spy! Henri thought, his mind moving quickly.

"He could have fooled us all along."

"Don't be silly, Henri," Sarah scolded. "I'm sure

Moses has a perfectly logical explanation." She turned to Moses. "You do have a logical explanation?" she asked hopefully.

Moses struggled to his feet and placed his arms at the base of his spine. "Oh, my back," he moaned in pain. "Of course I have a logical explanation," he assured Sarah. "I'm a Mechanic."

"Huh?" James asked. "What does that mean?"

Moses rubbed his back and sat down gingerly on a stack of newsprint. "The Mechanics are a secret group of patriots concerned about how Britain is treating the colonies," he explained.

"I thought that was the Sons of Liberty," Sarah said.

Moses shook his head. "Their membership is reserved for men of commerce. We craftsmen, having no group of our own, decided to form one. We call ourselves Mechanics."

Henri was skeptical. "I've never heard of them," he remarked.

James smiled. "Not being known can be advantageous for a spy ring," he told Henri.

Sarah looked curiously at Moses. "Why didn't you tell us about this?" she asked.

"Because these doings are not games," he replied with great seriousness. "There's great danger in simply knowing about these secret societies . . . to say nothing of knowing who belongs to them." Moses struggled to his feet. He was in severe pain. He was also a little angry. "Thanks to your enthusiastic defense of Dr. Franklin's print shop, my mission is in dire jeopardy." He reached into his pocket. "I was to deliver this urgent message to Dr. Joseph Warren, a colleague of Samuel Adams."

The children didn't have to ask what was in the letter. They could tell by the grim look on Moses's face that this was an important, urgent message.

And they were right.

"We have heard from our sources that the British army is moving out of Boston, to New York," Moses explained. "If the colonists are caught off guard, this could end in disaster. The colonists will see the British troops and think it's an attack. It's a powder keg." He grimaced in pain and rubbed his back. "And now I can't warn Dr. Warren."

James felt terrible. This was all their fault. "I'll warn him for you, Moses," he assured him. "Let me take the letter to Boston. I'm your man."

But Sarah was not in agreement. "And who says a woman cannot be part of this vital undertaking?" she demanded.

Henri wasn't about to be left out. He moved closer toward Sarah and James. "I'm going, too!" he declared.

Moses smiled at the brave little French boy. "Sorry, Henri. I'm going to need you here to help me get around."

"Aaaww," Henri said with a pout.

Moses looked at Sarah and James. "As for you two—"

"Moses, this message must be delivered," James interrupted. "You said so yourself. There is no alternative. You know I can do it."

"Well . . . ," Moses said, hesitating.

"*We* can do it," Sarah interrupted. "Two have a better chance than one."

"That is true," Moses agreed.

James narrowed his eyes. "But, Moses!" he exclaimed. "She's British!"

"Most of the colonists are British, James," Moses reminded the teen. "It's not about which side one's on. It's about saving lives."

Sarah nodded in agreement. "I may be British, but that doesn't mean I can't see both sides of the question. It's the violence and bloodshed I fear and hate."

Moses nodded in agreement and then turned to

James. "It's settled," he said, leaving no room for argument. "A ship leaves for Boston at dawn, bearing emergency supplies. I was to be on it. Now you two will go in my stead.

"Help, please . . ." He reached out his arms. Instantly the two teens grabbed his arms and pulled the injured man to his feet. "As for tonight, get some rest. All of you."

"Don't see why I have to rest," Henri grumbled as he followed the older children up the stairs. "I'm not going anywhere."

Chapter Eight

It had been more than a year since Sarah had been aboard a ship. But it didn't take long for her to remember how uncomfortable you could be traveling in cramped quarters over rocky water. Still, it was a relief for her to know that the trip to Boston from Philadelphia would last only a few days. The trip from London to Boston had taken nearly two months.

Not that this journey was much easier. The ship Moses had arranged for was tiny, and loaded with food and supplies. There was hardly any room for travelers. And spending so much time with James had been difficult. Although both teens were glad for the company, they'd gotten into their share of arguments along the way. Their beliefs were so different, and the lack of privacy and space didn't help, either.

So by the end of the journey, Sarah found herself spending a lot of time sitting quietly, keeping to herself. She used the time on the ship to think.

"Why so quiet?" James asked her one afternoon as the two teens sat near the bow of the ship, huddled together against the wind. "After all these long days and nights at sea, we're almost to Boston Harbor!"

"I'm worried," Sarah replied, whisking a strand of her windblown red hair from her face. "I hope I'm not committing an act of treason. What would my mother think?"

"We're saving lives," James reminded her. "That's not treason."

Before Sarah could answer him, the ship's captain came racing across the ship. "Stay down and hold on," he ordered the teens. "There be trouble ahead."

The captain may have ordered them to stay down, but James's natural sense of curiosity wouldn't let him do that. He peered over the bow of the ship to see what the problem was. Trouble wasn't even the word for it! "It's a British frigate!" James told Sarah.

Sarah gasped. A warship!

"If they catch us with contraband on board . . ." James began, his voice suddenly becoming frightened.

KABOOM! Suddenly, there was a flash of fire and a huge explosion as the frigate launched a heavy cannon-ball into the ocean. A splash of water as tall as a geyser whooshed into the air.

"They're firing on us!" James cried out.

The two teens held on for dear life as the tiny sailing ship shifted hard to the left. But the captain was in full command. In an instant the small ship made a radically sharp turn to the right. The frigate was much bigger. It couldn't make a turn like that. The Red Coats were forced to sail straight ahead, past the small ship.

"Don't worry," the captain told James and Sarah. "They're just warning us off. The harbor's still closed."

And what a warning. The frigate fired loudly again. *KABOOM!* A second geyser of water drenched the tiny ship as the cannonball hit the ocean.

"We'll lose them by staying in the shallow waters close to the coast, where they cannot go," the captain explained to the two drenched teens. "But we're going to have to put you ashore several miles south of Boston. I'm afraid you will have to walk the rest of the way."

☆ ☆ ☆

Walking would have been fine—had there been any roads to walk on. But when Sarah and James went ashore, they found themselves faced with bleak marshland.

Sarah made a face as she surveyed the muddy ground. "We have to walk through *that?*" she moaned.

"Unless you can sprout wings and fly," James replied. "Fear not, we're only two hours from Boston."

Sarah sighed, lifted her skirts, and began to trudge through the mud. James followed behind, slapping away bugs and trying not to fall in the mud holes. It was not an easy journey. It wasn't a short one, either.

"These wretched bugs," Sarah complained as she waved away a group of annoying gnats. She scowled at James. "Two hours, you said? It's been four, and

A British Frigate Firing upon a Sailing Ship

they've been the longest hours of my life."

James looked at the map of Massachusetts the ship's captain had given him. "Luckily, according to the maps, the road should be dead ahead." James looked off toward the horizon. Sure enough, he could see a cluster of gray wooden buildings in the distance. "See!" he exclaimed as he waded through a patch of soggy reeds. "There it is."

Sarah followed James through the weeds and then up onto a thick plateau of mud. She looked down at the soggy hem along the bottom of her dress. "Yuck," she moaned. "My dress is ruined."

"It'll dry soon enough," James assured her with a dismissive tone. "Let's eat. I'm starving."

Sarah reached into her woven traveling bag and pulled out a hunk of bread and some cheese. James did the same. The teens were so hungry, they couldn't seem to get the food into their mouths fast enough. Still, they quickly lost their appetites when they heard the thunderous sound of horses galloping toward them.

"Someone's coming!" Sarah gulped.

"We'd better hide," James suggested. "Who knows if they're friend or foe?"

Quickly, he dropped his sandwich and pulled Sarah into a clump of marshy bushes. It wasn't the most comfortable of hiding places, but it was the best available place at the moment.

James peered out from between the bushes. In the distance, he could see Red Coats approaching on horseback. "They're wearing uniforms! British regulars," he whispered to Sarah. "Get ready to duck!"

The officer leading the troops pulled his horse to a stop. "Halt!" he ordered the others. "Halt, I say."

The soldiers did as they were told, pulling back on the reins of their horses.

"I spy something on the ground there," the officer told his men. He pointed to the sandwiches James and Sarah had dropped. "Have a look, Sergeant."

The sergeant leaped from his horse and examined the evidence. "Bread and cheese, sir," he informed the officer. "Dropped here within the last few minutes, I'd wager. Not an ant in sight."

"Have a look around," the officer told him. "But be quick. We must join the others in Boston tonight for tomorrow's journey to Lexington and Concord."

The sergeant did as he was told, walking around the area and looking in the bushes for anyone suspicious. James and Sarah flattened themselves farther into the mucky shallow water behind the bushes. They didn't dare breathe. Sarah shut her eyes and tried to remain calm as the sergeant's sword swished through the bushes above her head. What a close call. Another few inches, and . . . Sarah didn't even want to think about it.

Finally, the sergeant gave up his search. "Nothing here," he reported to his commanding officer. "Nowhere else to hide. Perhaps there is someone on the road ahead of us."

"If that be so, we will catch up with them shortly. Come," the officer ordered.

In an instant, the British sergeant mounted his horse, and the patrol of Red Coats thundered off into the night.

James and Sarah stayed still, making sure that the soldiers weren't returning. Finally, after a few more nerve-racking minutes, they rose from the mud.

"That was close," James said, sighing.

Sarah wrinkled her nose. "That was *messy!* My clothes!"

James shook his head in amazement. How could Sarah be concerned about her clothes at a time like this? Hadn't she heard a word the British officer had said? "Sarah, the British are not going to New York at all! They're riding to Lexington and Concord! We have to tell Dr. Warren!"

* * *

Chapter Nine

* * *

Sarah stood in front of the gray wooden house and looked down at her dress. It was a mess—mud stained and torn. Without even so much as a glance in a looking glass, she knew that her face and her hair probably looked just as bad. The amused expression on James's face told her so. Not that he looked any better. He just didn't care.

Sarah knew this was no time to dwell on appearances. Still, she could give an attempt to clean herself up. As James knocked on the door, Sarah wiped her handkerchief over her cheeks. The white cloth became muddy brown.

The door opened. A refined Massachusetts gentleman of about forty-five years of age looked at the teens with concern. From the looks of them, it seemed as though there must have been a terrible disaster somewhere. "Dear heavens!" he exclaimed.

"Dr. Warren?" James asked.

"Yes. Yes. Was there an accident?"

"No accident, sir." Sarah blushed. "That's not to say we look this way on purpose—"

"Let me get to the point, sir," James interrupted. "We come from Philadelphia, with an urgent message from the Mechanics. But even more importantly . . ."

Before James could say another word, Dr. Warren eyed the boy nervously. "Hold on," he warned. "I'm not aware of any mechanics who send messengers. What sort of mechanic? Cobbler? Wagon maker?

Sarah and James looked at each other. Moses had made it clear that Dr. Warren would be expecting a message from the Mechanics. Things became clearer, however, when they heard the sound of soldiers marching up the street. The British were coming in the direction of the doctor's home.

"I cannot talk to you now," Dr. Warren said as he hurried to close the door.

"Wait!" Sarah urged him. "We're from the printer,"

she said, realizing that that must be Moses's code name in the group.

Doctor Warren stopped for a moment and eyed Sarah suspiciously. "Ah, and the printer's wife . . . how is she?" he asked.

James looked at Sarah curiously. He had no idea what this exchange was about.

But Sarah knew exactly what to say: "We both know he isn't married, sir."

Dr. Warren opened the door wide. "Come in," he urged. "Quickly." Sarah did as she was told.

But James was still trying to figure out what had just happened. "Huh?" he said.

Sarah rolled her eyes. "Don't dawdle, James," she said with an air of superiority as she rushed past him.

Dr. Warren ushered James and Sarah into his home and gave them a seat by the hearth. The cold, wet teens were glad for the warmth.

The doctor peered nervously out his window and then spoke. "I must apologize for my interrogation, but with all the spies around, one can never be too careful."

Sarah and James nodded and watched as the doctor stared out the window again. As soon as Dr. Warren was sure that there were no British soldiers nearby, he walked over toward the teens.

"Well now, you know who I am, but I don't know who you are—other than you've come from Dr. Franklin's print shop and Moses."

As the doctor spoke, James began to understand the strange conversation Sarah had had with him outside. He gave Sarah an admiring glance. "The printer," he said to himself. "Riiiiight."

"I'm Sarah Phillips," the girl introduced herself.

"James Hiller," James added.

"Please excuse the way we look," Sarah apologized. "We've been at sea for almost two weeks. And then we walked through an endless swamp to get here."

Dr. Warren was shocked. "You came all the way from Philadelphia?" he said.

James nodded. "Moses said our message was urgent."

"Hold on," Dr. Warren warned before James could say another word. He walked over toward a door that led to the dining room of his home. "There are some gentlemen who need to hear this," he added as he opened the door.

Dr. Warren peered into the room and beckoned two men to come into the room where James and Sarah stood. "James Hiller and Sarah Phillips," Dr. Warren introduced them, "Paul Revere and William Dawes."

"Call me Billy," the shorter, rounder of the men said.

Paul Revere nodded in the children's direction. "Pleased, I'm sure."

James studied the two men carefully. He had no idea who Paul Revere or Billy Dawes were. But he was certain that they must be important to the cause of revolution. Why else would Dr. Warren bring them into the room?

"James and Sarah have brought us urgent news from Philadelphia," Dr. Warren told the men.

James fished Moses's sealed letter from his coat pocket and handed it to Dr. Warren. Quickly the doctor snapped the wax seal and scanned the dark, handwritten message inside.

As the doctor read the note, James continued speaking. "What we've seen outside the city is more pressing, sir," James assured him. "Boston Harbor remains blockaded, and the British are on the move . . . but they are marching on Lexington and Concord, *not New York!*"

Paul Revere did not seem at all surprised at James's new discovery. "That confirms everything we know," he told the others. "Tonight's the night."

Dr. Warren agreed. "Yes, the rumors Moses heard about the British marching on New York are completely false. The rumors we heard, from the British groom, are completely correct."

The doctor angrily crumpled Moses's letter into a tight ball. There was only one reason the British would attack the cities of Lexington and Concord. That was where the colonists had been storing up their gunpowder and weapons. "The British are marching on Lexington and Concord—by sea—which means they'll be going after Samuel Adams and John Hancock, not to mention the colonists' stores of guns and ammunition," he added ruefully.

James gasped. He knew Samuel Adams well. He, Sarah, and Henri had worked with him in the past, helping to get pamphlets distributed to the colonists. And everyone knew who John Hancock was—the great patriot colonist who was helping to pay for many of the Continental Congress's expenses. This was awful. "Not Adams and Hancock!" he exclaimed.

"Not if we get there first!" Dawes assured him.

Dr. Warren threw Moses's letter into the fire. There could be no evidence of its existence. "We have no time to waste," he told the others. "Lives are at stake! We must move fast if there's any hope of preventing armed conflict."

Sarah was stunned. The thought of there actually being combat was almost too much for her to bear. She had a personal stake in seeing that such a thing never happened. "Armed conflict!" she exclaimed. "My cousin is with the British regulars stationed here. He's just doing his duty. Will he be in danger?"

"That's precisely what we're trying to avoid," Dr. Warren assured her. "We want no man to be in danger, be he British or Colonist."

Paul Revere nodded in agreement. "I myself have many friends among the Regulars," he told Sarah. "Let me assure you, if we can get Hancock and Adams to safety, bloodshed will be avoided on both sides."

"I pray you're right, Mr. Revere," Sarah said.

Dr. Warren placed his hat on his head and walked toward the door. "Thank you both for your efforts," he told the teens as he reached into his pocket. "I'd like to pay you something for your trouble."

James shook his head. "Very kind of you, sir. But we'd rather be of assistance."

Dr. Warren considered that for a moment. "Perhaps there is something else you can do," he said. But he did not volunteer any ideas. Instead, the doctor turned to Paul Revere and Billy Dawes. "We must get going," he told the men as they walked outside to get their horses. "Warn every volunteer from here to Concord. Wake them up. Knock on every door if need be."

Billy Dawes nodded. "I'll go by land, out through Boston Neck."

"Right," Paul Revere agreed as he buttoned his long black coat. "After I set the signal at North Church to let everyone know the British are coming by sea, I'll cross the river and arrange for a horse in Charlestown."

"It will be dangerous," Billy Dawes warned. "But if one of us meets with trouble, hopefully the other one will get through."

James leaned over to whisper in Sarah's ear. "We've got to be a part of this!" he murmured excitedly.

Sarah did not share his enthusiasm. "But James," she whispered back nervously, "I'm verging on treachery already."

James shook his head. "You're looking at it all wrong," he told her, making sure to keep his voice low so the men couldn't hear. "This is history in the making! Dr. Franklin needs us to observe! Otherwise, who will ever know what actually happened this night?"

That struck a chord with Sarah. It was important that people have information about what was going on in the colonies. And that information had to be honest, and unbiased—which was something James could not guarantee. He had trouble seeing both sides of a story. For that, he would need her help. "You're right," she admitted finally. "The truth must be told."

James and Sarah stepped closer to the men. "We'd like to come with you," James told Paul Revere and Billy Dawes.

At first, the men were surprised. But the idea seemed to grow on them.

"They would make good cover," Paul Revere mused.

"We'll help raise the alarm," James volunteered.

"I can be loud, Mr. Dawes," Sarah assured him.

"She can," James agreed, with a teasing lilt in his tone. "Breaks glass all the time."

Sarah shot James a dirty look.

The teens watched anxiously as Paul Revere and William Dawes exchanged glances, considering the possibility of bringing James and Sarah along.

Finally, Paul Revere nodded. "All right, then," he said. "Come along."

But Dr. Warren wasn't so sure this was a good idea. "Hold on!" he warned. "I don't know if Dr. Franklin would consent to my putting you two in danger."

"With all due respect, sir," Sarah said in her upper-class British way, "Dr. Franklin's right-hand man, Moses, did send us here."

"And Dr. Franklin is behind us one hundred percent!" James assured him.

"Philadelphia to Boston in just thirteen days," she told the doctor, reminding him of just how dedicated and crafty she and James could be when danger was afoot.

Billy Dawes was very impressed. "That's fairly flying!" he exclaimed. "I could use some of that!"

"Yes, you can," James agreed. "We're young. We can handle a midnight ride, sir."

Dr. Warren couldn't fight all four of them. He had no choice but to give his consent. "Very good, then. Godspeed. And write well. Tell the world of our gallant boys and their midnight ride to stop bloodshed."

James got into Paul Revere's carriage. Sarah got into the one belonging to William Dawes.

As James rode off with Paul Revere at his side, he could barely contain himself. This could be his biggest news story ever.

The teen looked up at the bright spring sun burning in the sky and sighed. It seemed as though midnight would never come.

Chapter Ten

Finally, the hands on the clock moved close to the twelve. Midnight was almost upon them. As James followed Paul Revere up the narrow, winding staircase of the Christ Church, his heart began to pound with excitement. It was beating so loud, he was certain Paul could hear it. But Paul Revere had other things on his mind besides James's heart. He was focused on lettting the colonists know the British were coming.

"Sorry to disturb you, Reverend Newman," Paul said as he greeted the Reverend Robert Newman, who was the minister of the church. "But the British are on the move, and they are preparing to cross the Charles River."

The Reverend Newman nodded. "Two lanterns, then?"

"Yes, just as we agreed," Paul confirmed. "One if by land, two if by sea. The whole city will be able to see them from the belfry."

James remained on the steps as Paul Revere and the Reverend Newman made their way to the cramped belfry that sat on top of the church. The teen watched as the men lit two lanterns and hung them where they could be seen by all.

Suddenly, James heard hoofbeats coming toward the church.

"Hello?" the Reverend Newman asked nervously. "What's that noise?"

Paul Revere opened the window of the belfry and leaned bravely over the side. A British patrol thundered by right under his nose.

Once he was certain the two lanterns were solidly in place, Paul Revere turned and began tiptoeing back down the stairs. He beckoned for James to head down the stairs with him. "Quietly," he warned.

Paul Revere slipped out through a side door of the church and walked quickly to his carriage. James was right on his heels. The two quickly rode off into the distance.

It didn't take long for the carriage to make its way

to the banks of the Charles River. There, James and Paul Revere boarded a small wooden rowboat that was waiting for them, with two of Paul Revere's most trusted friends already onboard, ready to row Paul and James across the river. As the boat moved swiftly across the river, James listened for the sounds of the oars splashing into the water. But the oars were completely silent. It took him a moment to realize why, but then he noticed that there thick pieces of cloth wrapped around each oar. "Petticoats to muffle the oars," he said quietly.

"Great idea. Too bad about the full moon, though. I feel there's a lantern on us." Paul Revere was worried about the full moon as well. Especially because the rowboat was not alone on the river. In the distance he could see the stern of a large British warship turning straight toward them. The name of the ship was written broadly across the side. "Shhh," he whispered ominously to James, "The *Somerset*."

James shut his mouth and sat completely still as the tiny rowboat slipped past the huge war vessel. Remarkably, the sailors on the *HMS Somerset* didn't seem to notice the rowboat at all.

Suddenly, James heard an unfamiliar voice calling out in the darkness. "Paul! Over here!" A tall, strong man waded out into the water to greet Paul Revere.

The "Somerset"

"Deacon Larkin, reliable as always," Paul greeted the man.

"I saw the lanterns," Deacon Larkin told him. He handed Paul the reins to his horse. "My father's horse, as promised."

"I hope she's fast," Paul said, taking the reins in his hands.

"Won many a race for me," Deacon Larkin assured him. He looked Paul in the eye. "Watch out for the Redbellies," he added with concern. "The roads are crawlin' with them."

Despite the seriousness of the moment, James found Deacon Larkin's use of the word "Redbellies" for the Red Coats pretty funny.

But Paul Revere didn't seem to notice Deacon Larkin's humor. He was more concerned with his mission. He tipped his hat in thanks and then mounted the horse. James climbed on behind him and hung on for dear life.

In a second, they were off to warn the colonists that the British were on their way!

As James and Paul Revere rode through the streets of Charlestown, just outside of Boston, Sarah was on the back of Billy Dawes's horse, fearing for her life.

The horse moved so quickly over the muddy road that Sarah had to hold on to Billy's waist, just to keep from being thrown. And that was no easy task, considering how wide Billy's waist was.

Suddenly, Sarah spotted some movement in the water far off in the distance. "Look! To the north!" she shouted in Billy's ear.

Instantly, Billy followed her line of sight and stared out toward the river. There he saw a whole fleet of rowboats making their way across. "Whoa!" he cried as he pulled on the horse's reins. The horse came to a stop, allowing Billy to get a good look at the action. "Good eyes, girl," he complimented Sarah. "I believe the British are crossing to Cambridge." He looked again. "Yes, it's the Regulars. We've no time to lose!"

Paul Revere

With a swift kick to the horse's side, Sarah and Billy took off once again. They, too, had to warn the colonists.

"Get up! Get up!" Sarah shouted as they rode through the streets. "The Regulars are heading this way!" Her voice was louder than she'd ever imagined possible. But she had to make sure the people of Boston heard her. Lives depended on it—her *cousin's* life depended on it!

"The British are on the move," Billy Dawes bellowed as his horse flew past a cluster of houses.

"*This* British certainly is," Sarah said to herself as she bounced up and down on Billy Dawes's horse.

☆ ☆ ☆

James's experience at that moment wasn't much different from Sarah's. He and Paul Revere were also dashing through the streets on horseback, shouting at the top of their lungs that the British were coming.

But suddenly, Paul Revere pulled back on the reins of his horse. The animal came to a dead stop, and Paul leaped off. He let out a sharp whistle and called out into the night, "John Hancock! Sam Adams! Bestir yourselves!"

Paul Revere gave James a reassuring smile. "Welcome to Clarke House, James. Known for its peace and quiet," he joked in a whisper. Then he raised his voice to a shout. "Sound the alarm!"

Almost instantly a sentry guard appeared in the courtyard. "Halt!" the sentry demanded. "People are sleeping here! Keep that noise down!"

"Noise!" Paul scoffed. "You'll have noise enough before long. The Regulars are coming! Help me wake the house!"

The sentry leaped into action, pulling a bell cord to sound the alarm. Paul Revere raced to the front door of Clarke House and began banging on the front door.

Suddenly a lantern was lit in an upstairs window. "Coming!" John Hancock shouted into the courtyard. "Don't break it down."

Within an instant, both John Hancock and Sam Adams appeared at the front door. They squinted in the moonlight, struggling to see who had awakened them so vehemently.

"What's going on, Paul?" John Hancock asked.

"John, Sam, the Regulars are on the move, and they mean to capture you two, and all the munitions they can find." The words spilled from Paul Revere's mouth without even a breath.

John Hancock and Sam Adams exchanged glances.

They'd known for a while that this might happen. They had a plan ready for such an occasion.

"We'll gather our things and repair to Buckman Tavern to plan our escape," John Hancock assured Paul Revere. Quickly, he and Sam Adams returned to the house and prepared to leave.

At that very moment, James heard hoofbeats in the distance. His heart froze. Had the Regulars arrived? Had he and Paul Revere been too late?

Chapter Eleven

Quickly, Paul Revere spun around to see who was approaching. The worried frown on his face reversed itself when he spotted Billy Dawes and Sarah ride into the courtyard, safe and sound.

"James! How was it?" Sarah asked excitedly as she leaped off the horse and raced over toward her friend.

"Incredible!"

"James," Paul Revere called over toward the teens, "take care of the horses."

"I'll help," Sarah said, taking Billy Dawes's horse by

the reins and leading him to the water trough.

"Mr. Revere's courage is amazing," James told Sarah. "When I tell the story, he'll be famous."

"But his is only half the story," Sarah reminded him. "Mr. Dawes has been doing the same thing, just as amazingly."

"I can only write what I witness," James told her in a dismissive tone. "And I've been with Paul Revere."

That made Sarah very angry. James always seemed to feel that his point of view was the only one worth reporting. She didn't say anything, but her expression let James know exactly what she thought of his arrogance.

So help me, from here on out I am going to become a reporter, she thought. *These events are far too important to leave to someone like James!*

Just then, Paul Revere and Billy Dawes made their way over to the trough. "Mr. Dawes and I are riding on to Concord," Paul told the teens. "We'll understand if you don't want to come."

"And miss the story of a lifetime?" James piped up. "Not me." He turned to Billy Dawes. "Of course, Sarah may want to stay," he added.

"Not a chance," Sarah assured him. There was no way she was giving this whole news story to James.

She wanted all points of view represented!

That settled it. Once again, James mounted Paul Revere's horse, while Sarah climbed on behind Billy Dawes. Then the four of them trotted off in the direction of Concord, Massachusetts.

"My horse is tired," Billy Dawes remarked as his horse slowed slightly. "She's had a long night."

"We all have," Paul Revere agreed.

But this was no time to slow down. There were hoofbeats in the distance. They were getting louder with each passing second.

Before Paul and Billy could even turn to see who was approaching, they heard someone call out their names.

"Revere? Dawes?" the man said.

"Aye," Paul Revere responded. He struggled to see who was heading their way. In a moment, he recognized the man's face. "Dr. Prescott, the freedom fighter?" he said.

"Call me Samuel," Dr. Prescott said. "I heard about your ride, Paul Revere, and I thought I'd join you."

Before Paul could answer, the thundering sound of soldiers approaching on horseback rang through his ears. The British had arrived!

"You, hold there!" a Red Coat officer demanded.

"Let's split up," Paul Revere suggested.

Samuel Prescott nodded. "See you in Concord," he assured Paul as he rode off into the night.

But William Dawes was not as quick to leave. "My horse will never make it," he explained to Sarah.

Quickly, she slipped from the horse's back, lightening its load. "It will now," she told him. "Go. They won't do anything to me. I'm a British citizen."

"You're also a brave girl," Billy Dawes praised her. Then, with a single kick to the horse's side, and a loud "Hyaaah!" he took off for Concord.

There was no way James was about to leave Sarah alone on the road. "If you're staying, I'm staying," he assured her as he hopped off the back of Paul Revere's horse. "Go, Mr. Revere, and good luck!"

Paul Revere shook his head. "You're in my charge," he told the teens. "The others will get the message through."

James opened his mouth to speak, but he was too late. The British patrol had closed in on them. There was no way out, now.

"You, what's your name?" a British officer demanded as he rode up beside Paul Revere and the two teens.

"Revere," he said proudly. "Paul Revere."

The officer and his sergeant exchanged triumphant glances. Paul Revere's name was well known to the Red Coats. Their soldiers' commanding officers would be thrilled that he'd been captured.

"Boston's famous express rider," the officer mused. "What brings you out tonight?"

Paul Revere didn't answer.

But words weren't necessary. With a single touch to the neck of Paul's horse, the officer could tell exactly what Paul had been up to. The horse's pulse was beating fast.

"I see you've been riding hard," the officer said. "Alerting the countryside of our regiments headed this way?" he wondered.

"I won't deny it," the brave man replied.

Paul Revere's pride in his actions angered the British officer. "Dismount, sir," he demanded, turning to his second in command. "Sergeant, take his horse. Mr. Revere, if you attempt to run, or we are insulted, you'll pay the price."

"You may do as you please," Paul Revere said.

Sarah and James were overwhelmed with admiration for Paul Revere's bravery. It was now time for them to be brave as well.

"What are you two doing out here?" the Red Coat

officer demanded of the teens. "Shouldn't you be in bed, leaving such treasonous activities to your elders?"

Sarah was outraged. "I've committed no treason," she insisted proudly. "I am a loyal British subject from a respectable English family."

"Oh, but of course. Pardon me for not recognizing you immediately, your ladyship," the officer said.

Sarah smiled triumphantly.

"It was the muddy face and dirty hair that had me fooled," the soldier added with a laugh.

Sarah's face fell. Her cheeks burned with shame. She straightened her clothes and quickly brushed a few strands of her long red hair from her face. But it did nothing to improve her appearance.

James sensed her shame. He put a gentle hand on her shoulder in a show of support.

But the officer wasn't at all touched by Sarah's embarrassment. "Sergeant, round up these urchins," he ordered haughtily. "We'll need someone to clean up after the horses."

Sarah blinked back tears as the soldiers laughed in her face.

Sarah, James, and Paul Revere spent the next few hours walking behind the soldiers' horses as the troops headed toward Lexington. It was a difficult hike. The stench of the horses was unbearable, and they had to be careful to avoid mud holes and horse droppings along the road.

Suddenly, a shot rang out in the night.

"Uh-oh! Trouble ahead," the British officer warned.

The sergeant was eager to join the action. "Can we lose the prisoners?" he asked hopefully. "They're only slowing us down."

"They're traitors," the officer reminded him. "They should be taken into custody."

"We're needed more ahead," the sergeant reminded him respectfully.

The officer considered that for a moment. "All right," He sighed. "Release them. But keep their horse. It's fresher than ours."

"Yes sir!" the sergeant replied enthusiastically.

The British officer turned and rode back toward Paul, James, and Sarah. "You're free," he told them. "I strongly suggest you go home. Don't let our patrols catch you on the roads again."

With that, the British patrol galloped off toward the sounds of gunshots in the distance. The second they were out of sight, Paul Revere turned and began walking across a muddy field. He, too, was headed in the direction of the gunshots. "Come," Paul called back to James and Sarah.

"Where are we going?" James asked.

"Back to Lexington. We have to help Hancock and Adams escape."

There was no arguing with that. Immediately, Sarah and James plunged their feet into the mud and began trudging across the field.

"What a story this will be!" James exclaimed.

Sarah looked down at her torn, stained dress and mud-drenched boots. "Worth every pound of mud, I'm sure," she murmured ruefully.

★ ★ ★

It was nearly dawn by the time Paul led the teens to the Buckman Tavern in Lexington, where Sam Adams and John Hancock were holed up. Paul Revere was anxious to help his friends find a safe haven. But this was the end of the journey for James and Sarah. It was too dangerous for them to be with the wanted men for any long period of time.

"Thanks for your help," Paul Revere told the teens sincerely. "You'll be safe here at the inn."

James thrust out his hand. "Thanks for letting us come along," he said. "All the world will know of your brave acts when our newspaper article is published."

A few hours later, after they'd bathed and eaten, James and Sarah sat by a fire at the inn. Despite the fact that neither teen had slept in more than a day, they were both wide awake, writing furiously in their notebooks.

"Got to get these notes to Dr. Franklin while tonight's events are fresh in my mind," James told Sarah with a yawn. He sounded every bit like the full-fledged reporter he so longed to be.

"I'll have a little something for you to include in your dispatch," Sarah told him. She pointed to a pile of papers, all filled with her neat handwriting.

"What is that?" James exclaimed. "A blooming novel?"

Sarah smiled triumphantly. "No, just the half of the story you left out. The truth must be told!"

Joseph Hosmer, the innkeeper at Buckman Tavern, wandered in and placed another log on the fire. "Up all night, warning the countryside that the British were on the march, it's a wonder you two are still standing," he remarked, looking out the window.

But as he turned around, he saw that the two reporters were far from standing. In fact, James was curled up in his chair and snoring slightly as sleep over took him.

Sarah took advantage of the moment. She pulled a fresh piece of paper from her sack and began to write once again.

19 April 1775

Dearest Mother,

Last night was the most exhilarating experience I have ever had. I rode along the back woods of Boston, warning the colonists that British soldiers had arrived in Lexington. It was my attempt to save lives, and keep war from breaking out in the Colonies.

But with the sun rising, the excitement of last night's ride is giving way to anxiety. The people of the colonies are stubbornly independent; never more so than here in Massachusetts. They are bent on governing themselves and now decry the very "Red Coats" who just twelve years ago helped them win the French and Indian War.

Chapter Twelve

Sarah tried to wipe the spilled ink from her letter. But the more she wiped at the black smudge, the worse it became. She put the letter away. She was too worried to finish it, anyway.

Her mind moved to Lexington, where the soldiers most likely had already arrived. Her cousin Tom would be among them. Would he be all right? Or would he fall victim to all this madness?

Cousin Tom, she thought. *He's serving under General Cage. Marching on Concord. What must he be thinking right now?*

Suddenly, Sarah had an idea. Maybe, just maybe, she could find a way to stop war from breaking out. It only took one person to make a change. Maybe that one person was her cousin Tom. She quickly began gathering her things.

The sudden movement in the room stirred James from his sleep. He sat up and rubbed his eyes. "Are you up already?" he asked Sarah. "What are you doing?"

"I'm going to find my cousin," Sarah explained. "What he's thinking is what the people of these colonies need to know. He has a lieutenant's perspective on the soldier's role in keeping peace."

James shook his head. "There won't be peace until we have the same rights every Englishman has," he said in a clipped, determined tone. "The rights we took for granted not long ago."

"James, these are the king's colonies," Sarah reminded him as she packed away her notebook and charcoal. "Is it reasonable to expect him to just let them disregard Parliament's laws?"

"Is it reasonable to send troops to enforce tyranny?" James countered.

Sarah kneeled down on the floor beside James. "The king doesn't want trouble any more than you do," she assured him. "But unless both sides understand one another, trouble is bound to come."

James nodded. "On that, we agree," he allowed. "But Parliament has ignored our petitions. It's now up to the king to make them understand. He has the power, if only he'd use it."

Sarah stood and picked up her traveling bag. "And that's why I'm going to see Tom," she told James. "So the colonists will understand that their 'fight' is with the lawmakers, not with the soldiers."

James leaped to his feet. A sudden sense of responsibility for Sarah's well-being came over him. "You can't!" he pleaded with her. "It could be dangerous."

Sarah nodded. She was fully aware of the gravity of the situation, and of the risk she was taking. "I expect it will," she agreed. "But this is a big story, with two sides, and you can't cover both at the same time. So we'll have to work together, irrespective of the danger. I'm off to find my cousin." And with that, she walked out of the inn.

Sarah's statement appealed to the reporter in James. There was a big story out there, and he wasn't about to miss it. "Wait a minute," James called to her as he rushed toward the door. "Sarah, I thought we were working together."

He peered out into the street. Sarah was already out of sight. "Darn!" James exclaimed. "Her 'together' is faster than mine!"

Sarah looked up at the sky as she walked along the muddy road that led to Lexington. It was past dawn now, and the sky was a rosy pink. Bells were tolling in the distance. Everything seemed peaceful. It was almost impossible to believe there was so much danger afoot.

But the calmness was soon destroyed by the sound of heavy footsteps coming up from behind her. Sarah turned to see a long line of Red Coats marching toward her. The company halted near a well that had been dug along the side of the road. Sarah rushed over to where the men had stopped and scanned their faces, hoping to get a glimpse of her cousin in the ranks.

"See to your water supplies," Colonel Smith, the leader of the troops, commanded. "Fall out."

As Sarah looked at the men, a sense of worry came over her. Most of them didn't look much older than she was. And yet here they were, carrying guns, ready to risk their lives. These were certainly unusual times they were living in.

Then, suddenly, a familiar face passed by. "Tom!" Sarah exclaimed. "Tom Phillips!"

A young man with a head of hair as red as Sarah's turned in the direction of her voice. His face brightened when he saw her. "Sarah!" he exclaimed. "Where . . . how . . . what are you doing here?" he stammered with surprise.

Sarah giggled and gave him a little shrug. "I'm hopelessly attracted to a man in uniform," she teased as she reached up and gave her cousin a huge hug. It felt so wonderful to see someone from home; to be with family once again.

Just then, a stout lieutenant walked over. "I'm a man in uniform," he said flirtatiously. "Introduce me, Tom?"

Sarah blushed so fiercely, her cheeks turned the color of her hair.

"This is my cousin, Sarah Phillips," Tom said politely. "Sarah, allow me to present Lieutenant Bryan Johnson."

"I'll save my greetings for someone less impertinent," she scolded Bryan Johnson.

But the lieutenant wasn't giving up. "I beg pardon, Miss Phillips," he apologized in a very flirtatious manner. "It's not every morning a beautiful young lady accosts us on maneuvers. Say, how did you know where to find your dear old cuz? You're not a spy, are you?"

Sarah didn't find that humorous. "I'm a loyal British subject, thank you," she assured the lieutenant. "I'm here to write a newspaper story." Her voice softened as she considered the fate these young soldiers were facing. "And to warn you that you and your company may be in grave danger."

"Don't worry," Tom assured her. "There'll be no trouble. General Gage himself said he 'doubts that the infernal rebels would take up arms against His Majesty's Troops.'"

Sarah wanted desperately to believe that. But after all those months of living among the colonists, she couldn't help but fear that General Gage was underestimating his opponents.

But before Sarah could offer that opinion, church bells rang out from almost every church in the area. The sound was deafening.

"Major Pitcairn, what do you make of all these bells?" Colonel Smith asked.

The major frowned. "They announce our presence, sir," he explained, "as surely as the scarlet and white of our uniforms."

"Fie!" the colonel complained. "This was to have been a secret mission."

"A vain hope, I'm afraid, sir," the major admitted. "I rather doubt we'll achieve our objective of confiscating the colonials' munitions."

"Cursed rebels," the colonel muttered. "We've

endured a sleepless night and tremendous discomfort on their account."

But in Sarah's eyes, Tom didn't look any worse for wear. He seemed older to her, more mature. "Soldiering suits you, Tom," she assured him.

"The finances back home left me no other choice," Tom admitted.

Sarah nodded. She'd heard that the economy back in London wasn't very good. Many people were out of work.

"Still, everything works out for the best," Tom continued. "I've done all right for myself."

"Every man here is proud to serve with him," Bryan assured Sarah, patting Tom on the back.

"But Bryan's the real soldier. These ragtag colonists will wilt when faced with the likes of him."

"In truth, most of the colonists remained loyal to the crown," Bryan told Sarah. "There's only a handful of troublemakers."

Sarah took out her pen and paper and began to write. "I'm pleased to hear you say that, Mr. Johnson," she said. "That's exactly the sort of thing my readers need to hear."

Just then, an officer on horseback raced up to Colonel Smith. "Colonel, the scouts report a number of armed rebels concentrating at Lexington just ahead," he reported.

Colonel Smith took a second to consider his options. Finally he turned to Major Pitcairn. "Major, you will proceed into the township with an advance guard," he ordered. "I shall follow with grenadiers. The rebels may be up to no good, perhaps not. We'll err on the side of caution. Dispatch your swiftest rider to General Gage. Have him send reinforcements. The cooler heads among the rebels will carry the day if we outnumber them."

★ ★ ★

Like Sarah, James found himself on the road to Lexington as well—researching his own news story. Already, he had come across three brothers, Robert, Jedediah, and William Munroe—members of the local rebel militia who had been in the tavern the night before, with Sam Adams and John Hancock. All three men were armed with muskets and ready to do battle. They seemed good sources for his story.

"Mr. Munroe, I'm James Hiller, a reporter for *The Pennsylvania Gazette*," he said, introducing himself. "I was wondering what militia this is, and who is in charge?"

"There are two companies here, James," William

Munroe explained. "Minute Company and Alarm. Our leader is up ahead, there at the green."

"And he would be?" James asked.

"A veteran of the French and Indian War, Captain John Parker."

James quickly scribbled down the captain's name, thanked William Munroe, and scurried off toward the green. He was anxious to speak to Captain Parker.

As James was approaching, the captain was attempting to organize his men into something resembling an army. "Gentlemen, please form into your respective companies."

But the new militia was filled with men who had never trained for battle. This group of shop owners, students, and farmers were volunteers, and unaccustomed to taking orders. They moved slowly into their companies, unlike the British soldiers who snapped to attention whenever an order was given.

James walked over to Captain Parker. "How about me, Captain?" he asked.

The commander looked the boy over. "You're welcome to join us, lad," he said. "But you'll need a weapon. I'm afraid we have none to spare."

James held up his charcoal pencil. "Here's my weapon," he told the captain. "I'd like to join as a reporter."

Captain Parker grinned. "A writer, printing the right things, is worth a thousand soldiers."

Suddenly James heard the sound of hundreds of soldiers marching up the hill. The British had arrived, and they greatly outnumbered the rebels. "You might want to amend that statement, sir," James said nervously.

Captain Parker stood tall, and readied himself for what was to come next. "Sound 'To Arms,'" he ordered his bugler.

A Bugle

* * *

Chapter Thirteen

Major Pitcairn led his men into Lexington. The Red Coats took position on the far side of the green. More than six hundred British soldiers were lined up, weapons at the ready. They were prepared for anything.

About fifty yards away, the colonists were also forming ranks. They didn't have fancy uniforms or well-polished guns, but they were there, lined up and ready to fight. Somehow they had gathered at a minute's notice—which was precisely why the colonial militia had been nicknamed the Minutemen.

Captain Parker walked over toward his men. The Minutemen had already scrambled into two rows.

"They number close to six hundred and fifty," Captain Parker told his second in command, Sergeant Munroe. "How many are we?"

"Fewer than eighty, John," Sergeant Munroe replied.

Captain Parker sighed. Those were not good odds. Should the fighting begin, the colonists would not stand a chance.

James was standing near Captain Parker. He, too, was surveying the enemy's troops. But his eyes weren't focused on the huge number of Red Coats facing him. His attention was on a tall, redheaded British girl standing in the middle of the sea of soldiers. "Sarah!" he exclaimed. Instantly he began to make his way over to her.

★ ★ ★

"You'll be perfectly safe here," Tom Phillips assured his cousin as he escorted her behind the stone wall, moments later.

Sarah looked at him suspiciously. "If you're under orders not to harm anyone, why do I need to hide?"

"It's just a precaution," he assured her.

Sarah moved behind the wall, but kept her eyes peeled on the green.

"Um, the wall will work better if you duck behind it," Tom suggested as diplomatically as possible.

Sarah did as she was told. She squatted down low, and kept her head behind the stones. She looked up at her cousin. "Should I be worried about you, Tom?" she asked.

"Not at all," he assured her. "Neither side wishes to fight. I'll see you shortly." Her cousin gave her one last encouraging look, and then left to return to his regiment.

Sarah waited a few seconds, until she was certain that Tom was out of sight. Then she slowly began crawling along the wall, searching for a crack. "Squatting behind walls isn't very dignified for a lady," she murmured to herself. "And it's useless for a reporter." After all, how could she witness what was going on on the green if she couldn't see it?

Finally, Sarah found what she'd been looking for: a small break in the wall that she could peer through. Sarah moved her eyes closer to the crack. She couldn't believe what she saw. "James!" she shouted out in disbelief. Sure enough, there he was, standing almost in the center of the green, looking at the British troops.

James's safety was not going to be left to chance any more than Sarah's had been. "Find yourself a safer place than this, young man," Captain Parker ordered.

"'Tis folly to stand here!" Joseph Hosmer, the innkeeper James and Sarah had met earlier, agreed.

But James stood firm, his pencil scribbling every word Captain Parker said as he addressed his troops. "Steady, men," the brave captain told the Minutemen. "Stand your ground and don't fire unless fired upon."

Suddenly, in the distance, James could hear a drum beating. The British soldiers began to march toward the colonists, their boots marching in time to the beat. Quickly, James darted behind a line of trees at the far end of the green, and watched as the British drew closer.

Major Pitcairn nudged his horse nearer to Captain Parker. He raised his sharp sword. "Lay down your arms and disperse, and you will not be harmed," he said in his clipped British accent.

But Captain Parker was not about to surrender. "Stand your ground, men," he told his small militia.

Major Pitcairn was dismayed. This was the last thing he wanted. He had hoped to stay away from violence. Still, if he could just find a way to stop the colonists from instigating any fighting . . . "Surround and disarm them!" he ordered his soldiers suddenly.

Sarah held her breath and waited. Would the

colonists do as they were ordered? Would they drop their guns and leave? "Please disperse," she whispered to herself. "Please do what the major says. Please don't let this get out of hand. . . ."

But the colonists were not about to give up their arms. Major Pitcairn had no choice but to force the matter. Still, he resisted any urge to call for gunfire. He merely wanted to frighten the colonists, and make them surrender without bloodshed. "Charge bayonets. Light Company advance!" he ordered.

Immediately the British began to march closer to the colonists. Captain Parker watched as a sea of Red Coats descended upon them. "Give way, men," he ordered his small band of soldiers. "Fall back."

The Minutemen did as they were told, backing away from the oncoming army.

"We do not want violence," Major Pitcairn told the colonists. "Lay down your arms."

"You'll have to take them!" Joseph Hosmer insisted.

By now, the Minutemen were fighting amongst themselves. Some wanted to turn back. Others wanted to stay and face the enemy. Some colonists were actually pushing and shoving one another. Captain Parker tried in vain to control his small army.

And all the time the British soldiers kept advancing.

"Surrender your arms," Major Pitcairn ordered

once again.

"We will not!" a colonist shouted back.

"We shall use force," a British soldier warned.

"You've no right," a Minuteman countered.

"Disarm them!" Major Pitcairn ordered.

Sarah watched in amazement as the British and the colonists engaged in a shouting match. But words were safe. At least there hadn't been any gunfire.

KABOOM!

Until now. Suddenly, a musket discharged in the field. Sarah's eyes scanned the crowd of soldiers, trying to see which side had fired that first shot.

But it was impossible to tell.

"Where did that come from?" Captain Parker shouted.

"Present arms! Present arms!" a British officer shouted, certain that the Red Coats were being fired on.

"No!" Major Pitcairn commanded.

It was too late. Both sides were certain that the other had fired the first shot. The British aimed their muskets. The colonists moved back, but their guns were at the ready.

Kaboom! Instantly, British soldiers began firing.

"Stop," Tom Phillips shouted at his fellow Red Coats. "We were ordered not to fire."

Major Pitcairn spurred his horse and galloped into

the ranks, his sword held low. That was the signal for "hold your fire." But the British soldiers paid their commander no heed. They just kept firing their guns.

Sarah watched, stunned, as Captain Parker and five other Minutemen dropped to their knees. Had they been shot?

James, who was watching from behind the trees, wondered the same thing. But as he looked up from his notes, he saw six colonists aim their muskets to return the fire.

The British Regulars were surprised. Not for one instant had they dreamed that the colonists would ever return fire. But they had underestimated the Minutemen. What they lacked in numbers, they made up for in passion.

"They're firing!" a British officer shouted out. The men around him began reloading their muskets.

Bryan Johnson reached over and grabbed his friend Tom Phillips's shoulder. "Tom, we're being shot!" he cried out. Then, suddenly, the young soldier stumbled in pain. Tom caught his friend in his arms.

As Tom struggled to find out where Bryan had been hit, bullets soared overheard. A new regiment of Red Coats, alerted by the sound of gunfire, had arrived at the green as well, eager to support Major Pitcairn in battle.

But Major Pitcairn didn't want help in battle. He wanted the shooting to stop. "Hold your fire!" he cried out again. But the shots kept coming.

Captain Parker called out to his men, as well. "Fall back!" he shouted.

The Minutemen did as they were told, dropping their weapons and fleeing for safety as fast as their legs could carry them. They were no match for the hundreds of well-trained British soldiers on the Lexington green, and they knew it.

But for some of the colonists, the retreat had come too late.

How many soldiers were lost in that battle? Ever the reporter, James risked his own safety to find out. He ran from his safe haven in the trees and joined the shell-shocked Minutemen in their retreat.

"Cease fire. STOP FIRING!" James could barely hear Major Pitcairn's voice over the sound of gunshots.

A single voice could not stop the fighting. But Colonel Smith was certain that a chorus of British drums could do the trick.

"Sound 'To Arms,'" he ordered his drummers.

Immediately, five British drummers began to beat out the familiar rhythm.

Within seconds, the Red Coats ceased their firing. They went silent, waiting for their next order. The only sign of movement on the green was the cloud of gun smoke wafting over the grass.

"Shoulder your firelocks!" Major Pitcairn commanded.

Instantly, the British soldiers fell into ranks.

The Battle of Lexington had ended.

Chapter Fourteen

The Battle of Lexington may have come to an end, but there was no doubt in Captain Parker's mind that the fighting would continue in Concord, the British army's next destination. And *that* could only lead to more colonists giving their lives for freedom.

"Does anyone know how many casualties there were?" the captain asked his men as they walked slowly, painfully, along the road to Concord.

"Eight dead, sir," James shouted as he jogged to catch up to the captain. "A number of others wounded. I couldn't count them. I was . . ." He stumbled over his words, mortified at his own feelings. "I was afraid."

Captain Parker put his hand on James's shoulder. "Nothing to be ashamed of," he assured the teen. "We all ran."

"Who fired first?" James asked.

"It doesn't matter," Captain Parker said, with more than a touch of regret in his voice. "It has brought us to war."

James took a moment, trying to let that register in his mind. *War*. It was a small word, but its effects would be enormous. He took out his pencil and jotted down a single thought.

A war no one wanted.

★ ★ ★

No doubt the Minutemen were discouraged by the Battle of Lexington. The British soldiers, however, were rejoicing in their victory—most of the soldiers were, anyway. Major Pitcairn was more than a little dismayed by what had happened. "I'm sorry for these disagreeable circumstances, Colonel Smith," he apologized to his superior officer. "The men show little inclination for discipline."

Colonel Smith did not agree. "Do not deplore the actions of your men without first examining your own, Major," he countered. "We are here to seize munitions, not kill colonists. There had better be no such display in Concord."

Before Major Pitcairn could respond, a soldier raced to his side. "We've a man down," he reported.

Colonel Smith and Major Pitcairn turned to see a cluster of Red Coats around the fallen soldier.

"Surgeon!" Major Pitcairn called out.

The surgeon came running. So did Sarah Phillips. Sarah was certain that her cousin Tom had been hit. "Tom?" she cried out as she pushed her way to the center of the crowd of soldiers. "Tom?"

Suddenly, a strong hand touched her shoulder. Sarah turned quickly. Her eyes gazed on a familiar face, that of her cousin Tom. He was shaken, but not injured.

"It's Bryan," Tom told her. "His leg is badly shot."

Sarah watched as the British doctor bandaged Bryan's leg, trying to stop the bleeding. Thankfully, Bryan seemed to be feeling no pain as he lay unconscious on the ground.

As soon as the dressing was completed, four Red Coats lifted Bryan from the ground and carried him from the green. It was the last Sarah saw of him.

"Form ranks!" Major Pitcairn cried out.

Tom bent down and picked up his musket. He moved to rejoin his fellow soldiers.

"Tom, please don't go," Sarah begged. Tom had been lucky this time, but there was no guarantee that in Concord he might not wind up like Bryan . . . or worse.

Tom took his cousin's hands in his own. "I must," he said simply. "It's my duty."

"Then I'm coming with you," Sarah insisted.

"I don't think you should," Tom told her. "Things could become dangerous from here on out."

"Don't try to talk me out of it," Sarah warned him. "A war may have started here today. I'm going to cover the story start to finish. And you're going to help me."

"Present arms!" Colonel Smith's voice rang out over the green.

The British soldiers raised their muskets in the air and fired a victory volley. "Huzzah! Huzzah!"

"We march to Concord," Colonel Smith ordered.

"Huzzah! Huzzah!" the men cheered again as the company moved out. Major Pitcairn sat on his horse and watched as his men marched down the road in a sea of red jackets. He shook his head ruefully. "What have we done?" he asked. "What have we done?"

Chapter Fifteen

"Where are we headed?" James asked as he hurried to catch up to Joseph Hosmer and the other colonists.

"To the liberty pole," Joseph replied. "Major Buttrick's giving orders. He's a good man. We fought side by side against the French and Indians during the last war."

James followed the Minutemen down the long, muddy road to Concord. As they marched, they were joined by men from all over the surrounding countryside. By the time the Minutemen arrived in the center of town, they were 250 strong!

The men stood in a mob around the tall, wooden liberty pole. It was the perfect meeting spot—a symbol of the colonists' determination to be free.

Major Buttrick addressed the disheveled, but dedicated troops. "The rumors are true," he told the men in a serious tone. "The Red Coats have shot and killed militiamen in Lexington—"

Libery Pole

"Two of my kinsmen among them," Sergeant Munroe interrupted. The crowd roared in anger.

"Now they're headed here to Concord," Major Buttrick added, knowing full well the response a statement like that would bring.

The militiamen did not disappoint.

"The men of Acton await your orders," a militiaman from Acton, Massachusetts, assured the major.

"As do the men of Lincoln," another soldier said.

"The Meriam's Corner are ready," cried another.

"And Bedford," added another.

"Excellent!" Major Buttrick smiled. "We'll need

every man to help defend our liberties! Follow me!" he ordered as he began to march out of the center of town and toward the North Bridge.

James was worried. He knew the violence could not be stopped now. There was sure to be fighting in Concord. Sarah was with the British troops. She could be in real danger. Quickly, James ran up beside Sergeant Munroe. "Sergeant, I have a friend, a fellow reporter, who's with the British," he explained in a worried manner. "Is there a way we can tell the men not to shoot at her?"

Sergeant Munroe shook his head and held up his musket. "They won't aim for a woman," he assured James. "But these muskets are not accurate at a long distance. They could hit anybody, or miss anybody."

As the sergeant marched on with the other militiamen, James thought, *I hope that "anybody" is not Sarah.*

✷ ✷ ✷

Sarah stood alongside her cousin Tom and the other British Regulars as they set up a command post in a graveyard on a hill, high above the center of Concord. From there, they could see the militiamen clearly as they marched toward battle.

"Look at them, how brazen!" Colonel Smith said

as he surveyed the 250 colonists marching out of the town and toward the bridge. "They're not even trying to conceal their strength from us!"

"They've given us the center of town. Perhaps they want no more trouble," Major Pitcairn suggested hopefully.

"Neither do we," Colonel Smith reminded him. "Let's not forget General Gage's orders that the people of Concord are to be treated with respect."

Tom and Sarah walked over toward the major and the colonel. "Colonel Smith, sir?" the young lieutenant asked respectfully.

The colonel stared at the two teens. They did not look familiar.

"Lieutenant Tom Phillips, Sir," he introduced himself. "And this is my cousin, Sarah Phillips. She's a reporter."

The colonel eyed the young, spirited redhead suspiciously. "Is that so, Miss Phillips?" he asked.

"Yes sir," Sarah assured him. "For *The Pennsylvania Gazette.*"

The colonel's suspicion turned to pure distrust. "Ben Franklin's newspaper," he remarked.

Tom stepped closer to Sarah, as a show of support. "Sarah is a loyal British subject, here to tell the British side of the story, sir."

Sarah quickly picked up on Tom's cue. "I believe that the majority of people here are loyal to England and supportive of the army's presence," Sarah assured him. She watched as the colonel's mouth raised into a slight smile of approval. "But there are those who would paint you as monsters," she continued. "I wish the colonists to know that the army is just as human as they are. And Mr. Franklin has allowed me to do that."

Colonel Smith nodded slowly. "You do have a way with words," he told Sarah as he led her to a chair with a view overlooking the town of Concord. He handed her a long telescope. "Allow me to offer you an excellent seat and a spyglass so that you can witness my gentle-handed discipline of the rebels in comfort."

"Thank you, sir," Sarah said.

Colonel Smith turned to leave. "Lieutenant," he said to Tom, "you are dismissed."

"Uh . . . yes, sir," Tom said as he turned to follow the colonel.

Sarah gave her cousin a cheerful wave. As he walked away, she looked through the spyglass at the crowd gathered below. She scanned the faces of the colonists, looking for one in particular. "James, James," she said softly. "Where are you?"

Chapter Sixteen

James stood a few yards from Concord's North Bridge and watched as the Minutemen took their positions. His pencil never strayed from his pad as he feverishly took notes.

"You there!" a deep voice called out in the teen's direction.

James turned to see Major Buttrick looking in his direction. The teen pointed to himself, unsure.

"Yes, you," the major assured him. "Come here."

James did as he was told. "Yes sir?" he asked.

"I'm lacking a spyglass," Major Buttrick explained. "May I make use of your youth and sharp eyes to give me a report on the British activity?"

James nodded. "I'll do my best, sir," he said as he looked up toward the British on the hill.

✷ ✷ ✷

The British officers were busy studying a map of Concord. "I dispatched four companies to search the Barret farm for hidden munitions, and two more to guard the North Bridge," Major Pitcairn told Colonel Smith.

The colonel seemed pleased. "Excellent!" he exclaimed. "What happened in Lexington must not be repeated here in Concord. These rebels need to be taught a lesson."

The major nodded. "May I suggest a symbolic gesture?" he asked mysteriously.

Of course James could not hear what the two British officers were discussing. He could only watch as they studied their maps. He was surprised as anyone when, a short while later, Major Pitcairn and several Red Coats approached the colonists' liberty pole and chopped it to bits with British axes.

Major Pitcairn had no doubt that the colonists would be furious at such an act. That was precisely the reaction he'd wanted. His act was designed to show the colonists who was boss. Liberty poles were symbols of their desire to break free from British tyranny. It was Major Pitcairn's feeling that they had no place in British territory. And that was exactly what the colonies were.

"That should send a message," Major Pitcairn remarked as he watched his soldiers throw the broken pieces of wood on a fire. "Quaint as they are, these liberty poles encourage rebellion. Burn it along with the gun carriages we confiscated."

Instantly, the soldiers threw wooden barrels and gun cartridges onto the fire.

As Major Pitcairn had suspected, the Barrett's farm had been the hiding place for many of the colonists' arms. He and his men had raided the farm and confiscated them all.

As he threw a piece of the liberty pole onto the fire, Major Pitcairn felt a sense of accomplishment. Surely the colonists would learn their lesson now. They could not outsmart the British army.

While Major Pitcairn and his troops burned the liberty pole and munitions, other Red Coats prepared to meet the Minutemen on the North Bridge. Tom Phillips was among them. As he and the other young soldiers marched across the wooden planks, they could see a black cloud of smoke rising from Major Pitcairn's bonfire. But these young soldiers were too busy to focus on a bonfire made from discarded arms and chopped-up pieces of liberty pole. They were far more concerned with the huge number of colonists who had arrived in Concord.

"There must be hundreds of rebels out there," Captain Laurie remarked with surprise. "And more pouring in all the time."

"The British army has fought against greater odds throughout the world and has repeatedly won out," Tom assured him.

Captain Laurie nodded, but he didn't seem very sure. There certainly seemed to be a lot of colonists—far more than there had been in Lexington. The battle there had obviously motivated the rebels. He sighed. "Nevertheless, I'll breathe easier when those four companies come back from the Barrett's farm."

☆ ☆ ☆

James was the first of the colonists to see the dark cloud over the town. "There's smoke coming from the center of town, sir," he warned Major Buttrick.

Joseph Hosmer looked back toward where the liberty pole had once stood. He pointed to the huge coils of smoke billowing in the air. He didn't realize that this was a contained bonfire. Rather, he thought the British were up to something far more severe. "Will you let them burn down the town?" he demanded, shouting at the top of his lungs. "I say we go put a stop to it."

His request was greeted with angry shouts of agreement. The Minutemen had had enough. They refused to let the British burn Concord to the ground.

Major Buttrick tried to calm his men. But he, too, believed that the town was in danger of being destroyed. The Minutemen had no choice but to come to the rescue of the people of Concord. "All companies, march to the bridge," he commanded. "But hold your fire. We'll not fire on the king's troops unless we're fired upon first."

The colonists fell into formation. At once they began marching down the hillside toward the bridge.

✳ ✳ ✳

Their movements were not lost on Captain Laurie. From his vantage point on the bridge, he could see every move the colonists made. "If they want the bridge, we'll give it to them." He gave a sinister smile and added, "In pieces. Fall back, men, and destroy the planking."

The soldiers did as they were told. Quickly, they began tearing away at the wooden planks in the hopes of destroying it before the colonists could arrive.

But the British soldiers weren't quick enough. The colonists were almost at the bridge. Any minute now there was sure to be a showdown between the two forces.

"It's no use, Captain," Tom told Captain Laurie. "We don't have time."

As the colonists came into view, one of the Red Coats fired a warning shot into the air, trying to alert his fellow regulars that the colonists were approaching.

The British soldiers readied their weapons and took aim. But still the colonists did not retreat. They just kept marching toward the bridge . . . all 250 of them.

KABOOM! The Red Coat soldiers shot off their muskets. Smoke clouds formed in the air above their heads as they fired on the colonists.

But still, the Minutemen kept marching toward the bridge. The Red Coats had shot first. Now they, too, had their muskets at the ready.

"Fire, for God's sake," Major Buttrick cried out to the militia. "Fire!"

And fire they did—directly at the British. The Red Coats fired back. And men began to fall.

✷ ✷ ✷

Sarah sat in the graveyard on the hill, watching through her spyglass. She could see the soldiers firing on one another. She could see men dying before her eyes. Her whole body began to tremble. Tom was down there. And James. She had to go to them.

"Tom!" she cried out as she leaped from her seat and raced down the hill. As she ran toward the battlefield, streams of Red Coats ran toward her, rapidly making their way back up the hill to safety. Running for their lives, the defeated British soldiers didn't even seem to notice the trembling teenage girl. They bumped into her and pushed her to the side in their cowardly hurry to get away from the Minutemen's bullets. The Regulars had nothing on their minds but saving their own skin.

Sarah frantically searched the faces of the retreating soldiers as they raced past her. "Tom!" she cried out. "Tom!"

But Tom was nowhere to be found.

That was the moment James spotted Sarah. She was running toward him, looking in every direction. She seemed so busy searching that she didn't even notice she was in the line of fire. James had to do something, fast! "Hold your fire!" James begged the Minutemen at the top of his lungs. "Stop shooting."

But one teen's voice was no match for the sound of blasting muskets. The soldiers couldn't hear him. They kept on firing their musket, right in Sarah's direction. And then, suddenly, James saw Sarah fall to her knees. Oh, no! Had she been hit? Quickly, he ran to be with her!

★ ★ ★

But it wasn't Sarah who had been hurt by the colonists' bullets. Instead, it was her cousin Tom who lay dying on the North Bridge. Sarah was kneeling beside him, cradling his head in her arms.

"Don't worry, Sarah," Tom said in a weak, distant voice. "This was all just a misunderstanding. Hopefully, we've ended the agitation here."

Sarah nodded hopefully. "Yes. Yes," she assured him as tears fell on his tattered red jacket, mixing with his blood. "Everyone will see what has happened and not want any more bloodshed."

"That's right," Tom said in a voice no louder than a whisper. "Everything works out for the best." His head turned to the side, and his body went limp.

Tom Phillips was dead.

Before the reality of it all had a chance to sink in, Sarah heard her name being called out above the sound of gunfire. She glanced up and, through her tear-filled eyes, spotted James running toward her.

"I'm glad you're all right," James said, looking at her sad, pained face.

Sarah stared back at him. Her heart was filled with both grief for her cousin and relief that James was all right. She looked back at Tom's motionless body. "My . . . cousin . . . Tom . . . " she whimpered.

James helped Sarah to her feet and gently led her away from Tom's body. "Come, let's go to a safer place," he urged. But as he listened to the gunfire around him, James knew that now that war had started, no place would be completely safe for any of them.

19 April 1775

Oh, Mother,

It is with a heavy heart that I must write you today. My beloved cousin Tom Phillips was killed in battle this afternoon. He died in my arms, and I shall never forget him.

The grim reality of Tom's fate seems a symbol of the war that will inevitably follow these dire events. The conflict is not at all what James thought it would be. It won't be simply a contest of ideas; it promises to be a contest of arms. It promises to be everything I had prayed we would avoid.

Your loving daughter,
Sarah

Chapter Seventeen

News of the Battles of Lexington and Concord spread quickly through the colonies. The newspaper story James and Sarah wrote for the *Gazette* became standard reading in Philadelphia and throughout the colonies.

But news took much longer to reach Europe— nearly two months, usually. This explained why, when Benjamin Franklin finally arrived back on the shores of his beloved city, he had no idea that war had broken out in the colonies.

As Dr. Franklin stepped off the boat in the Philadelphia harbor, he took a deep breath and looked out on the

calm waters of the Delaware River. "Philadelphia."
He sighed. "At long last."

Moses spotted his employer right away. "Dr.
Franklin! Dr. Franklin!" he shouted out excitedly.

Dr. Franklin walked down the gangplank and
greeted Moses with a hearty hug. It had been quite a
while since the two men had seen each other.

"How's London?" Moses asked.

Dr. Franklin sighed. "London is far away—both
geographically and politically," he said.

"I have news for you, Dr. Franklin," Moses said
quietly. He planned to tell the great patriot of the
battles in Massachusetts, but before he could, Dr.
Franklin told him news of his own.

"Moses, I used to love England," Benjamin Franklin
said. "Its beauty, its culture, its people. I had hoped
we could find a compromise under which the
colonies and the crown could coexist peacefully. I
even bought a home in London." As Dr. Franklin
looked into Moses's eyes, the anger rose up inside
him. "But Moses, I and our interests were met with
indifference, disrespect, contempt. Being in England
convinced me that a fight between the colonies and
the crown is now inevitable."

"Being here would have convinced you of the same

thing," Moses assured him. "Dr. Franklin, British soldiers fired on our people at Lexington and Concord!"

Benjamin Franklin's eyes opened wide behind his small glasses. The anger had nearly consumed him. "The crown's men fired upon her own subjects? Unthinkable!" he shouted. "Tell me everything, Moses."

Moses handed him the most recent copy of *The Pennsylvania Gazette*. Dr. Franklin's brow furrowed as he read the headline:

THE SHOT HEARD ROUND THE WORLD

by James Hiller and Sarah Phillips

"I'm very proud of them," Dr. Franklin said as he read the teens' report of the battles in Massachusetts. But his pride was tempered with a sense of sadness and determination. "And now," he said, "we must prepare for war."

YANKEE DOODLE NOT YANKEE AT ALL

by Sarah Phillips
Lexington and Concord, 1775

There's a new song being sung in the colonies these days. It's called "Yankee Doodle," and the colonists have proudly claimed it as their own victory song.

But truth be told, "Yankee Doodle" was actually made up by the British Regulars—to poke fun at the colonists. They said a Yankee Doodle was a backwoods hick who didn't know the first thing about fighting. In fact, some witnesses say they could hear the British drummers and pipers playing "Yankee Doodle" as their regiments marched to Lexington and Concord.

But the British are now singing another tune. After their devastating losses at Concord, the Regulars have a new view of the colonists. And the colonists have adopted "Yankee Doodle" as their own. As one Minuteman said, "We be Yankee Doodles, and proud of it!"

SENIOR SURRENDER

by James Hiller
Concord, April 1775

There have been many victory stories coming out of Massachusetts this past April, but none more surprising as the one involving Mother Batherick, an elderly woman who lives just outside Concord. On the day of the Battles of Lexington and Concord, all the young men of her town became Minutemen, and rushed off to join the Patriots in their battle against the British. This left behind the old men and women of the town. The old men were given the responsibility of guarding the town, under the leadership of David Lamson, a veteran of the French and Indian Wars. Lamson and his men were hiding behind a stone wall when some British supply wagons rolled by. Lamson asked the British Regulars to stop. But the Red Coats kept on rolling. Lamson and his men had no choice but to shoot. Two British soldiers were killed by the old men.

The six remaining Red Coats feared for their lives and ran to where Mother Batherick was digging weeds in a nearby pond and surrendered to her. Not knowing what else to do, Mother Batherick turned her new prisoners over to David Lamson and his troops.

All this begs the question: If one old lady can capture six Red Coats, just how many soldiers will King George need if he wants to capture America?

DATE DUE

Sarah Phillips

James Hiller

Benjamin Franklin

Henri Lefebvre

Moses